THE SLAVES OF HEAVEN

The only beings in the settlement that moved
were the Night Comers. They were dragging
unconscious women from the huts by their
legs and by their arms. He saw Vron, hauled
like meat, like the carcass of a fat deer, to lie
with the others. A Night Comer dragged her
out of the chief's hut, holding her by an ankle.
Her shift was pushed up over her belly,
exposing its roundness. The Night Comer did
not seem to care. He seemed totally indifferent.
Berry was filled with rage and anguish. For a
moment or two he was tempted to climb down
from the watch tower and fling himself upon
these silver monsters who had shamed him for
ever by dismissing all his defences, all his
precautions, with utter contempt. But reason
prevailed. What effect could an injured man
have on ten or more of these superhuman
creatures who had already defeated the entire
Londos people?

**Also by the same author,
and available in Coronet Books:**

The Slaves of Heaven

Edmund Cooper

CORONET BOOKS
Hodder and Stoughton

Copyright © 1975 by Edmund Cooper

First published in Great Britain 1975
by Hodder and Stoughton Limited

Coronet edition 1978

Printed and bound in Great Britain for
Hodder and Stoughton Paperbacks, a
division of Hodder and Stoughton Ltd.,
Mill Road, Dunton Green, Sevenoaks,
Kent (Editorial Office: 47 Bedford
Square, London, WC1 3DP) by
Richard Clay (The Chaucer Press), Ltd.,
Bungay, Suffolk

ISBN 0 340 22337 5

One

BERRY LAY CONTENTEDLY AGAINST Vron, savouring the
sweet smell of her body, methodically kneading her large,
hard breast as he sucked out the unwanted milk. Vron
yielded a great deal of milk, being greatly a woman. She
made far more than little Vron would ever take; and,
for the time being, the clan did not have any other babies.
It would be a pity to waste the milk. It would be a
crime.

He glanced at Vron's face. Her eyes were closed, her
lips were open. She seemed happy. He slipped his hand
between her legs and began to fondle her. She gave a
low groan of pleasure, but did not move.

Little Vron, sitting on the warm summer grass by the
side of her father and mother, observed the entire
operation with innocent interest. After a few moments, it
reminded her that she, too, was entitled to take milk. She
crawled to Vron's other breast, imperiously pushed away
the soft doe-skin that covered it and groped possessively
for the nipple. She found it.

Vron shivered joyfully. Then every muscle in her body
seemed to relax. She whimpered with sheer ecstasy. Her
man was on one side, her child was on the other. She
did not think of herself as a milch cow. For a time,
she was mother to the world.

Presently, Berry realised that he had emptied the
breast. He kissed Vron on the lips. She tasted her own
milk, and was amazed at its sweetness.

"It was good?" she asked, knowing what the answer would be.

"It was good, very good." Berry's fingers were creating devastation between her legs, but she did not want him to take them away. She knew he would not take them away.

He laughed. "I have given hunger to the little one."

"To me also," said Vron, opening her eyes.

Again he laughed. "Then I will satisfy your hunger as you have satisfied mine."

"Berry, let the little one finish."

"Then she must finish soon," he said. "There are things which do not keep well in the warmth of the sun."

Berry sat up, plucked a blade of grass and began to chew it. He was content. Why should he not be content? Since the death of Amri, two seasons ago, he had been chief of the clan. He had a woman of his own — no one else had — and he had a girl child. True, a boy child would have been better. But a man cannot ask for everything to come his way. It was against the laws of nature.

Still, thus far the gods had been very kind to him. No! I will not think that, he told himself fiercely. I don't care what the old ones believe. There are no gods, there is no heaven in the sky. These are dreams fit only for children, not for grown men. There are only natural things — things we know. The sun, the moon, the stars. The seasons. Wind, rain, snow, ice. Rivers, lakes, oceans. And the living creatures that dwell on the earth and in the air and in the water. Hunger and love, and death and birth. These are natural things. These are things we can understand. There are no gods! Who has ever seen a god? Who has ever returned from heaven to tell us what it is like? There are no gods.

But there were the Night Comers.

"Your forehead is wrinkled, Berry. Are you unhappy?"

"No. I am thinking. That is all."

Vron gave an indolent sigh. The baby still pleasured her by taking prodigious quantities of milk from her swollen breast.

"Thinking is hard. Do not weary yourself, my man. The sun is warm. Little Vron is almost finished."

"Good."

Vron could never understand that thinking was not an arduous task for Berry, but a form of relaxation, a kind of pleasure. Vron did not like to think. Why should she? She was a woman with much milk in her breasts, a child at her side, the promise of more to come, and with the chief of her clan for a mate. She was in clover.

What did that mean?

It was a saying the old ones used. Berry knew what clover was. It was a tiny plant with three round leaves, not good to eat. To find a four-leaf clover was supposed to be a sign of good omen. But what did the words mean? What was the point of being in clover if you could not eat it as a food that would enable you to survive?

Yet Berry realised that he, too, was in clover. He was not a blood member of the Londos, but he was now chief of the clan. The Londos had found him abandoned as a baby in the forest. His face had turned black and puckered like the skin of the sweet black berries that were good to eat when trees began to cast their leaves. He had been near to death. But there had been a woman of the Londos people, Mari, with breasts full of milk and a recently dead boy child to mourn.

Mari had given him her milk; and because his face was like the black berries, she had called him Berry. Mari had been taken by the Night Comers when Berry had been with her only seven summers.

He remembered the scene vividly. He remembered the

7

ordeal. He could not move. He could not cry out. Nor could anyone else. He could only watch Mari being dragged away, like a piece of meat, by the silver-clad Night Comers.

The image had been burned into his brain. The Night Comers were real because he had seen them. Gods and heaven were not real because no one had ever claimed to see gods or to return from heaven. But the Night Comers were real. And they had to be men. A strange kind of men, but still men. Not gods, but men.

They took women. Women only. So they had to be men.

"Little Vron has finished," said big Vron. "I am ready for you, Berry."

He looked at the baby. Asleep, now, drunk upon milk, mouth wide open. She had fallen from the breast in a state of stupor.

"And I am ready for you, Vron," he said, feeling the flesh between his legs grow painful with desire.

He sank the aching flesh into her. And she sighed, and groaned with the pleasure of receiving it.

He fondled her, caressed her, held her breasts savagely and took great pleasure as a residue of milk squirted up into his face.

But even as his seed pulsed into her body, he was thinking of the mystery of the Night Comers.

Two

THE LONDOS PEOPLE WERE not numerous. Nor were they warlike. They would fight if they had to, but only if there was no way of avoiding battle. Some of the other clans — particularly the northern ones, the Manches people, the Jords and the Glaskas — made fighting their way of life. They fought chiefly for women, being constantly short of women because the Night Comers took more or less equally from every clan. And who could stand against silver ghosts?

But, despite all the strange stories, Berry remained convinced that the Night Comers were not ghosts, as he was also convinced that they were not gods. It was known that they always wore silver garments. It was said that their very look could freeze a man, as if he were held in ice, so that he could not move a muscle for many hours. But it was said also that they had no faces, no heads. So how could creatures with no faces freeze a man simply by looking at him?

It was said that these faceless beings took the women they captured to heaven. But that was old men's talk, children's talk, women's talk. There was no heaven; and the Night Comers were only men with strange skills, men who needed a constant supply of women. Perhaps, Berry thought, they have no women of their own. That is why they must steal ours. So, if a way could be found to stop the Night Comers from stealing women, they would die out. For, he argued, without women to breed

9

from, any clan — no matter how skilful its men were — was doomed.

That is why, since he had become chief of the clan upon the death of Amri, Berry had devised an alarm system. It consisted of a long, thin, barely visible cord that was placed round the encampment at night, supported at about a leg's length from the ground by forked sticks five paces apart. If anyone or anything pressed against the cord, attempting to pass, a metal bell would begin to ring. Berry was very proud of the bronze bell. It was plunder — a souvenir of one of the rare occasions when the Londos had engaged in battle and had defeated a strong force of Jords.

So far, the bell had warned only of the incursion of wild dogs, pigs, a wounded bull and a stag that had obviously been hunted all day and was half out of its mind with fear. The Londos called the alarm system Berry's dog-bell. But they were glad of its existence. Since it had been brought into use, the Night Comers had not stolen any women. Perhaps that was an omen.

Berry, himself, did not place much faith in his alarm system. He knew it was crude, but it was the best he could devise — for the time being. He thought also that, if the Night Comers were as skilful as he surmised, they would find a way of taking the women they required without causing the bell to ring.

But the bell would have to be used until he could think of something better. Meanwhile, it gave the clan a sense of security. And that was something.

The Londos people were nomadic. They had been nomadic for generations, though their wanderings were restricted mainly to the south country. Like every other tribe or clan, they knew the hot spots and avoided them sedulously. Men who sought refuge in the hot spots — clan outcasts, criminals, those whose minds were unclear

— did not usually live long. Or, if they did, strange things happened to them. They developed horn or bone where there should only be flesh. They grew limbs where there should be no limbs. They went blind or began to see what others could not see.

Best of all, particularly in the summer, the Londos liked to stay close to the sea. The sea was bountiful. It gave forth an abundance of food — crabs, lobsters sometimes, cockles, mussels, many kinds of fish. If one had to choose gods, thought Berry, the sea would be one of the best gods of all. It was the source of much life, much food. Unlike the land, the sea was untainted. There were no hot spots. Or none that were known.

Berry was even thinking of building a permanent settlement near the sea. But it would need careful preparation to convince the clan that this was a good thing to do. Not only was the wandering way of life in their blood, but it was reinforced by a belief that to live permanently in one place brought disaster.

According to legend, the hot spots had once been huge settlements containing many, many clans. According to legend, these people had been greatly skilled in magic. They did not need to hunt or fish, or collect mushrooms, nuts, apples, berries and other things that were good to eat. Their magic, so the old ones said, had been so great that they could make food as they required it. Also they were supposed to have been able to make light and heat without the use of fire, so that it mattered not to them when the sun went down or when winter came; for they could create their own night and day and their own seasons at will.

But, the tellers of tales maintained, their magic was of no avail when the ground became too hot. It grew hot because too many people lived and walked upon it and spent all the days of their lives in one place, never journeying to unspoiled land to make a new camp. And when the ground became hot, pestilence came, destroying the great settlements, making the land on which they had been built unfit to be used by men for evermore.

Berry did not believe in magic; but he was half inclined to believe that the hot spots might once have been great settlements with far too many people. Perhaps these people did have strange skills. Perhaps, as was said, they could turn night into day and winter into summer. But not by magic. And perhaps they did not fully understand the nature of the skills they used. And very likely that was why they perished.

However, and whatever the truth about the hot spots might be, it would be difficult to convince the Londos that a permanent settlement was a good thing. Difficult, but not impossible.

Berry himself was aware of all the practical arguments for and against. The arguments against were: if you stayed in one place, you would soon exhaust the surrounding countryside of its game and its edible plants; your limbs would become weak because you did not constantly harden them by travelling; your women would spend too much time sitting around, chatting and making mischief because they did not have to engage in the hard work of setting up camp or getting ready to move on; and, finally, the ground would become hot because too many people walked upon it. But, also, there were strong arguments for staying in one place. You could build permanent weather-proof dwellings so that winter would not take its toll of the very old and the very young; you could devise fortifications for additional protection against other clans and the Night Comers; you could have fires that never need be put out; you could plant seeds of things that were good to eat; you could build boats and go out fishing whenever the sea was calm; and, in short, you could live better and more comfortably than was possible if you were constantly on the move.

Unless the ground became hot . . .

But Berry did not seriously believe that the ground could become hot because too many people lived and walked upon it. Besides, the Londos were a small clan. Even if the tellers of tales were right, it would take the trampling of the feet of many large clans to make the ground poisonous. And that could not possibly happen for generations.

So, one day, when the time was ripe, he would convince the clan that it would be a good thing to make a permanent home close to the sea. Then they would be able to make the best possible use of the food provided by the sea and the land. They would be able to stop living upon the edge of disaster, the edge of starvation. The Londos would be able to grow.

These thoughts passed through Berry's head as he lay close to Vron in the darkness of their doe-skin tent. Through small gaps between the loosely laced flaps of the doorway, he could see the stars dimming as the black sky slowly faded into grey. Soon the sun would rise and the day begin. He sighed. Another day when he would have to make decisions that might turn out to be good or bad but that only he could make because he was clan chief.

Amri had been stabbed to death because he had made too many bad decisions. Every man in the clan — including Berry — had thrust his dagger into Amri. It was the way of the Londos. It was barbaric and cruel, but it was practical. You could not peacefully depose a chief and choose a new one because, then, some would support the old chief and some the new. And the clan would be weakened.

So the privilege of being chief carried a built-in death

sentence with it. Few chiefs died of old age. Long before then they made too many bad decisions and were rewarded by the daggers of their people. The Londos were not vindictive. For the safety of the clan, they needed a chief who, on the whole, would make wise decisions. While he did so, he was assured of absolute loyalty and absolute obedience.

The Londos had long memories. They compared the performance of every chief with that of his predecessor. As long as he did as well or better, he lived. That is why not many men aspired to chieftainship. It was easier and safer to obey and then to criticise, rather than assume responsibility.

When Berry was elected chief upon the death of Amri, he was totally surprised, because he was not a Londos by birth. He had been found in the forest, near to death, his skin black with hunger and privation. Then he understood why he had been chosen. It would be easier to kill a stranger if he made bad decisions than to kill someone with strong blood ties in the clan.

But Berry was an optimist. He was young, and he felt that it would be a long time before he began to make too many bad decisions. Perhaps, before then, the customs of the Londos could be changed . . .

Berry always woke very early. It was a habit of many years. It gave him time to think tranquilly before the events of the day could cloud his judgment.

Soon, they would ask him whether the tribe should move north or south, east or west.

Meanwhile, he snuggled close to Vron, felt her buttocks against the top of his legs, felt desire rise between his loins. He placed a hand on her breast, but not urgently enough to waken her. She snored a little in her sleep. Her own arms lay protectively round little Vron who lay on her other side.

Berry gazed through the opening between the tent flaps and saw that darkness had gone. Daybreak was imminent. He thought of rolling Vron flat on her back and easing the aching between his legs.

Too late. Little Vron would cry, or the watchman would come. Or both.

Decisions!

The watchman came.

He made much noise to announce his coming. That was the custom.

"Chief, it has been a quiet night. Do we travel or do we stay?"

Berry stretched himself. Vron remained fast asleep.

"We stay, watchman. The weather is warm, the hunting is still good. We stay."

"So be it, chief. A good morning to you. I will tell the clan."

A good morning indeed, thought Berry. Since he had decided that the Londos would not move this day, there was no urgency. He could roll back to Vron and let his hand lie heavily enough upon her breast to wake her.

He did so. She still snored a little, but her buttocks moved and her breast twitched. Soon she would be conscious enough to receive him.

He hoped that little Vron would not be disturbed. But, if she were, would it matter?

Three

IT WAS THE RAID by the unknown clan — unknown because they carried no clan mark on their foreheads or their arms — which brought Berry close to the daggers of the Londos. And it was Oris of the thong-stones who challenged Berry's leadership. Oris was a reckless man, and greedy. More powerful of build than Berry, and less cautious. Also, it was known that he greatly desired Vron. Like any other man, he could demand, in his turn, a coupling with any woman of the clan. Any except the chief's woman. That was the custom of the Londos.

But Oris did not choose to couple with any other woman. He preferred to let his desire and his rage grow slowly. Berry had always known that there would come a time when Oris would challenge him. He had not expected it quite so soon.

The opportunity was given him because the unknown raiders — quite possibly they were Jords or Manches who feared reprisals if their clan marks were seen — had stolen five women and had killed or grievously wounded nine men.

At the fire-talk, Berry was covered in blood — the blood of his friends and clansmen. It was the custom for the clan chief to dispatch by his own hand those whose wounds were too grievous to heal quickly. Berry had performed the duty several times before; but usage had not hardened him to it. This time he had had to give the death stroke to Vron's brother, Riel, a boy with no beard

16

on his face, who suffered the loss of an arm and had an arrow through his stomach.

Berry could remember the day Riel had been born — a winter's day with snow packed against the walls of the tents and deep upon the ground. Not a good time for child-birth. The woman had died quickly, but the child had lived. In the Londos, as in any other clan, there was always some woman with milk to give. Riel had grown up to be tall but slight of build. Not much use as a fighting man or a woodsman, but a great singer of songs.

He would make songs about anything — about death, about birth, about the seasons, about the killing and the choosing of a chief. He had a pure, clear voice, full of confidence and joy. He used to cough somewhat in the cold months, and then he could not sing. But in the spring and summer, the voice of Riel had added greatly to the pleasures of evening, when hunting and journeying were done and, for a while, men and women relaxed, ate meat and fruit, and saw visions in the fire.

But Riel would sing no more. And he had not been singing when Berry looked at his thin, pale body and nerved himself to perform the duty of a chief. Riel had been whimpering and moaning like a baby while the life's blood drained from him. He had recognised no one, nothing.

He had not heard when Berry said softly: "Good night, song-maker. You will sing to us no more. But now, so they say, you will go to sing in heaven among the stars."

Probably he had not even felt the dagger that pierced his heart and released him from pain.

But now Berry stood before the people of his clan at the fire-talk, with blood on his hands and body, the blood of enemies and friends, and felt weary.

Oris sensed that his chief was dejected also, and was determined to make the most of this temporary weakness.

The fire-talk was a ritual that had grown in importance with the passing of the years. When Berry was a child, the fire-talk had been chiefly a social occasion, a time for exchanging ideas and opinions, for discussing the day's hunt or the day's march, for apportioning women to the men who desired to couple with them.

But in recent years, particularly under the chieftainship of Amri, who had never asserted great authority over the clan, it had become a time of criticism, a time of inquest, a time of trial.

The men — which is to say all males who had survived twelve summers or more — sat round the fire in a circle, while the women and children stood behind them in the shadows. As was customary, the chief stood close to the fire so that all could see him. As was customary, any man who wished to question or challenge the chief or address his fellow clansmen stood by the fire also, so that he, too, could be seen by the entire clan.

Berry and Oris were facing each other. Berry was weary and covered with blood. Oris felt strong, and there was no blood upon him. While Berry was dispatching the wounded, he had had time to wash away the stains of battle. He thought it was a good thing to appear without bloodstain before the man who had had to send several of his own clansmen to heaven.

"Berry, my chief, have I served you well or ill?"

It was a good beginning. Berry, also, knew that it was a good beginning.

"You have served me well, Oris. You have served the clan well. Today, as I recall, you slew two of the raiders. It was skilfully done."

"Then, chief, perhaps you will forgive a poor clansman for asking why you did not decide to travel this morning. If we had travelled, there would have been no raid; and some who are now in heaven would have been present at this fire-talk."

Berry sighed. "If we had travelled, there might still have been a raid, Oris. And if we had been on the march, our losses might have been yet heavier."

Oris shrugged, glancing confidently round the circle of firelit faces.

"Who can say, my chief? If we had marched early, the raiders might not have found us, or might not have been able to follow."

"That is true," agreed Berry. "But we stayed because the hunting is good here, and the weather is warm, and it was my decision to stay."

"Yes, chief, it was your decision." Oris turned to the circle of men. "I have no quarrel with Berry. I think only of the clan. In the early days Berry was a great hunter. He slew as much game with the javelin and the bow as I slew with my thong-stones, and I am no mean hunter. When he first became chief, he made us travel hard and hunt hard. He made many good decisions. But I say that Berry has now become soft. He hunts little. Perhaps that is because he is chief, and our chief is not required to hunt. Or perhaps he spends too much time with his woman, which, as we all know, weakens a man. Perhaps it weakens a man so that he can no longer make good decisions."

The circle was silent for a while, and tense. The men knew what Oris wanted, but there were those—particularly among the older ones—who liked Berry precisely because he did not drive them too hard.

"Are you asking us to make Berry embrace the daggers?" It was Ulbi who spoke. Ulbi was the oldest man in the clan.

Berry noted the warning sign. Normally, Ulbi would

have called him chief. But at this fire-talk he had become simply Berry once more.

"I speak only what is in my mind, Ulbi," said Oris cautiously. "There are times when a man must speak what is in his mind."

"That is true, Oris. So I, Berry, chief of the Londos, will speak my mind also. Perhaps I made a bad decision, perhaps not. I cannot say, nor can Oris. It may be that the raiders would have attacked us as we marched, it may be that they would never have found us. We shall never know. I have tried to make good decisions. A man cannot do more. It is true I do not hunt as much as I used to do. As Oris says, a chief is not required to hunt. A chief is required to think and to look after his clan. I do my best; and in this, at least, my heart is easy. Oris, though he does not yet say so, wishes for a show of hands. You know our custom. If many hands are shown, I will embrace the daggers. If few hands are shown he who challenges will undergo the same fate. I have no quarrel with Oris. He is a great huntsman and a valiant fighter. With him, I grieve for those we have lost this day."

Berry gazed at the circle of intent faces. "What you have to ask yourselves is not whether I made a bad decision—we all know that there has never yet been a chief who made no bad decisions—but whether you have fared well or ill while I have led you. Have I done better than Amri would have done, or worse? Make up your minds. That is all I have to say."

There was much muttering, much whispering. It was the whisperers whom Berry feared. They were the ones who were secretly trying to decide if they were strong enough for a show of hands.

"I have no quarrel with Berry," repeated Oris virtuously. "I think only of the good of the clan. It may be that a new chief would lead us better. But I have no quarrel with Berry."

"He has no quarrel with Berry! Oris lies!" A figure had leaped from the darkness over the ring of men and stood revealed in the firelight as Vron. She tore at the lacings of her doe-skin shift, exposing both breasts, swollen once more with milk, swollen and proud, darkly golden in the light of the fire. "These are his quarrel with Berry. My body is his quarrel as all here must know ... Well, Oris, you may call for a show of hands, and it may be that Berry will embrace the daggers. But you will never embrace these or me!" She gazed wildly at the circle of men. "Further, the first of you that raises his hand against my man will be dead before daylight. This I swear. If I live, it shall be."

Oris stared at her, hypnotised, like a rabbit confronted by a snake. He, the hunter, the warrior, the man who had challenged his chief, stood open-mouthed with astonishment, not knowing what to do. His weakness was noted. The whole clan saw it.

Berry, too, was discomfited. He also, did not know what to do or say. He tried desperately to collect his wits. He decided to pass the situation off as a joke. He turned to Vron and smiled at her.

"Woman," he said lightly, "with a defender such as you, I can fear no enemy. You have deprived Oris of his wits and you have struck terror into the heart of every man here. Go now to your tent before you commit further mischief."

"Yes, my chief," she said in a docile voice. "You sent Riel, my brother, to Heaven?"

"I did, Vron. He was sorely wounded ... If, truly, there is a heaven, then that is where Riel now sings."

She kissed his bloodied face. "I thank you for that kindness." And she went from the circle.

Berry looked at the firelit faces, and shrugged. "I am sorry. Who can say what passes in the mind of a woman?"

There was much laughter. The laughter of relief. Suddenly, Berry sensed that Vron's intrusion had turned the tide of feeling. Most of the Londos men were now for him. He knew it.

He glanced at Oris. Oris was still stupefied by what had happened.

"I am sorry for this—this happening," said Berry. "But perhaps we needed to smile and laugh somewhat. It has been a bad day, and there is much heaviness in all our hearts."

Oris had collected himself sufficiently to realise that he had been made to look foolish. The realisation kindled his anger.

"It was a bad decision," he shouted. "The woman, Vron, taunted me to make you all forget that it was a bad decision. Berry is no longer fit to lead the Londos!"

As soon as he had uttered the words, Oris realised that it was a mistake. The mood of the fire-talk was now against him.

"Well, then," said Berry tranquilly, "do you demand a show of hands?"

"I do not. The fire-talk has been cheapened by the mouthing of a woman who foolishly sought to preserve what she was in danger of losing. Berry hides behind the words of his woman. I will not seek him there. Let us to our tents, and think on it tomorrow. In one thing, at least, I can agree with Berry. The day has been a bad one." Oris made to leave.

"Stay," said Berry. "Oris, I have said that I am sorry for the words of Vron. Your words are harsh. Do you still not wish for a show of hands?"

"No. I have spoken my thoughts. It is enough."

Berry sighed. "Matters cannot be left like this. So I must call for a show of hands." He faced the circle of men. "Men of the Londos, charges have been made against your chief. Oris, who is a great hunter and a great warrior, has made these charges. Raise your hands now, if you wish to show me that my time is done and that I must embrace your daggers."

No hand was raised. Two hands were half-raised, but fell quickly when no support seemed to be forthcoming.

Oris was left alone. He was not without courage. He raised his right hand defiantly. "I call all here to bear witness that I did not ask for a showing, also that I remain true to my thoughts."

Berry did not relish his victory. "Oris, it was always known that you are a brave man. By custom, your life is forfeit — as mine would have been if the showing had gone against me."

"I know. I am not afraid. I go to heaven but a little time before you, I think. I will wait for you. Then we will discuss this matter further. In heaven, we are told, there is only one chief, to whom all must submit."

Ulbi, the old one, stood up and went to stand beside Oris.

"Let us not speak of heaven," said Berry. "Too many of our comrades have gone to that place this day. You are a great hunter and a valiant fighter, Oris. I do not seek your blood. The clan needs such men as you; and it is in my province as chief to grant you the right to live. More, I would make you, under my command, master of defence of the clan. And, in time of strife, I, too, would submit to your orders. Is that enough?"

Two more men, and a fourth, got up and went to stand beside Oris.

Oris was amazed at Berry's words. "Chief, it is more than enough."

I have miscalculated, thought Berry sadly. It has been a bad day, and I am tired. They will interpret my words as weakness. Soon the hands will be against me.

"I will accept —" Oris got no further. Swaying, he stared in amazement at the dagger Ulbi had thrust into his belly. It was followed by another dagger and then by two more. Oris sank to his knees, still trying to speak, but failing.

"Forgive us, chief," said Ulbi gently. "If Oris had lived, he would have divided the clan. There lies great danger. We understand why you tried to avoid bloodshed. But, sooner or later, there would have been another reckoning, which might have cost more than the death of one."

"Ulbi," Berry managed to say, "you have the wisdom of many years. You are right. I thank you."

Oris had fallen now to the ground. He was in his death throe. The firelight showed the sweat and pain on his face, the blood on his body. He was still trying to say something. But the pain obscured his words. He gave a great sigh and became still.

"The fire-talk is ended," said Berry. "I command you to take the body of Oris to lie with those who died this day in defence of the clan. Tomorrow, whatever the day brings forth, we shall travel. I have spoken."

He waited until Oris had been taken away, until the rest of the men had dispersed to their tents.

Then he went quietly away from the fire, out into the darkness, and was sick.

He took a strange satisfaction in the bitter taste of vomit in his mouth. He looked up at the stars, and marvelled that they could not weep for the plight of men.

Four

BERRY GOT HIS PERMANENT settlement. Despite all the known arguments — that the men would become soft, that the women would make mischief, that the ground would grow hot — he got the clan to agree before the leaves had fallen from the trees. He had already chosen the place. It was by a river. The sea lay not far away to the south. Wooded hills rose not far to the north. This was rich country, the best Berry had seen. The hills would yield game, the sea would yield fish. And, from the settlement, men might journey inland or down to the sea in their boats.

The settlement would be at least partly built before the first snows came. Which was good for many reasons, but chiefly because Vron's belly was swollen once more; and there would be another one to claim her breast in the spring.

Berry got his settlement because, during the warm months, the clan had suffered attacks as it had never suffered them before.

Marauding bands — all male — of Manches, Jords, Brumis and clans that Berry had never even heard of came south, all bent on stealing women, whatever the cost. Most of the groups of raiders were outnumbered by the Londos three or four to one. But they did not seem to care how many of them died, if only they could take women.

The clan was not frequently attacked because Berry

made too many bad decisions. Everyone came to realise that, though there were still those who thought secretly that Oris would have made a better leader. But Oris was dead somewhere in the forest, his bones whitening, and his spirit — no doubt still full of indignation — making the best of things in that heaven which was described by the old ones as the great settlement in the sky. Whereas Berry, leader of his people, slew many raiders in their defence, giving a good account of himself not only as a chief but as a fighting man whose javelin had once stopped three Jords with one throw.

He took prisoners, wishing to learn why the Londos had been more heavily attacked in the warm season than any living man could remember. He soon discovered why. The Night Comers had been more active than ever before. They had concentrated their attention mainly on the northern clans, and they had taken many, many women. So each clan that had been robbed had first tried to make good its losses by stealing from the nearest tribe. But, so the prisoners said, there was not a clan or tribe in the north that had not suffered at the hands of the Night Comers. To steal from each other under such circumstances would soon result in mutual destruction. So small groups of men who had little or no hope of obtaining women in their own country had journeyed south to take what they could before the Night Comers turned their attention to the southern clans.

Berry listened to the tales of the prisoners and marvelled at the sudden change of tactics of the Night Comers. Previously, they had cropped the clans as good hunters crop herds of deer and wild cattle, leaving enough does and cows to ensure that the herds would not be greatly diminished for future seasons. But now they seemed bent upon a course that could only result in the eventual shrinking of the clans — perhaps, even, in their extermination. Formerly, the Night Comers had been regarded as an infrequent affliction, to be endured with fortitude and resignation. Now, it seemed, they were fast becoming a threat to the very existence of the clans.

Berry wondered why. In the quiet hours of the early morning, while Vron snored peacefully by his side or grunted as the little one inside her kicked to take his exercise; in the quiet hours, before Berry was besieged by the problems and decisions of the day, he wondered why. If the Night Comers really wished to destroy the clans who supplied them with women, did this mean that they could be sure of a continuing supply elsewhere? Or that they could now afford to take all the women they could find because, by the time the clans died out, they would in some way be independent? Or that they did not really need all the women they took but that, in some way, they saw the clans as a threat and were using this means to reduce them?

Such questions were, for the time being, unanswerable. It had been several seasons since the Night Comers had last visited the Londos. But it was plain that they would return soon.

That is why Berry was able to persuade the clan to agree to a permanent settlement that could be properly defended. The threatened loss of the women was greater than the fear of the ground growing hot. If, as Berry argued, the ground showed signs of becoming hot, the clan could always move. But, if the women were taken, the clan was doomed anyway.

Further, he was able to persuade the clan to adopt the prisoners taken, instead of killing them. They were, he argued, good fighting men capable of helping to defend the Londos women. And if they were worthy of defending the Londos women, they were also worthy of coupling with them. As a demonstration of his good faith, and to ensure the loyalty of the new clansmen, he made Vron available for coupling, along with the rest of the Londos women.

Vron protested mightily. But she, like Berry, knew that it was no more than a gesture. The seed of the chief was already implanted in her belly. No man could usurp it. She opened herself for one of the new clansmen who had the temerity to choose her. But she ensured that he would never wish to be with her again. There were ways. Woman's ways . . .

So Berry got his settlement, built on the banks of a river, between the wooded hills, where deer and cattle and wild pigs roamed, and the sea, whose harvest was plentiful. The settlement was heavily defended with a deep ditch, sharpened wooden stakes, sentinels who watched through the night, and a bell alarm.

But all that was to no avail when the Night Comers struck.

Five

IT WAS A CLEAR, frosty night. The stars hung like points of cold fire in the black dome of the sky. There was no wind. Everything was still. The moon was full and bright, bathing all things in its silvery glow. At such a time, a man might believe fancifully — if he were alone as Berry was — that the entire world was frozen in a silver death and that he only retained the power of thought and movement.

Berry, wrapped in sheepskin, was taking his spell of duty in the watch tower. He was rather proud of the watch tower. It was his own invention, his own design. It was a small platform, walled and with a thatched roof, standing on legs that had been the trunks of four pine trees, each being six times the height of a man.

Since he had learned of the increased activity of the Night Comers, Berry had been greatly occupied with ways of making the Londos settlement proof against any attack. He had ordered that all shrubs and trees within a hundred paces of the settlement be cut down. And he had commanded the watch tower to be built in the very heart of the settlement, so that one man from this lofty position could have a clear view of the river and of the surrounding countryside. He had further ordained that the watch tower should be manned at all times and that every man, including the chief, should take his turn of duty.

So, now, here he was on a winter's night, cold despite

his sheepskin, mindful of the gratifying warmth of Vron of the swollen belly, who lay waiting for him in a warm hut that smelled of coupling and cooking, of life and of babies. Here he was, blowing upon his hands to keep them supple, glancing briefly and wistfully at the stars, searching the landscape anxiously, waiting for Sengo the Jord, the man who had chosen to lie with Vron and would never choose to lie with her again, to relieve him when the edge of the sun came over the eastern trees.

Berry had had his dog-bell installed in the watch tower. It had seemed a good thing to do now that there was a large, properly fortified settlement. The bell hung — none too securely, though Berry did not yet know that — from two thongs attached to the roof beam. One end of another thong was attached to the striker, and the other end was fastened to the platform floor, so that the bell would not ring when the wind blew. If the man on duty wished to give the alarm, he had only to pull the striker thong vigorously from side to side. This simple arrangement had been tested several times, and Berry was satisfied that everyone in the settlement could hear the bell when it was rung. What he had yet to discover — somewhat painfully — was that the strips of leather fastening the bell to the roof beam had become worn to breaking point.

The sky was already becoming a little grey in the east, heralding the approach of dawn. The stars were getting dimmer. Berry wondered greatly about the stars. It was said that they were hot, like the sun, but much farther away. It was said that the sun also was a star — a near star — which seemed a reasonable notion. But if that were so, why did the other stars go away in the daytime? Berry had thought about that long ago and had worked out what seemed a satisfactory solution. In daylight the other stars were still there but they could not be seen because of the brightness of the sun. But the moon, being very near, could sometimes be seen in daylight. Berry maintained that if a man did not have his eyes dazzled by the light of the sun, on a very clear day he would be able to see stars in the sky.

When he explained this idea to others, they received it with great good humour. But they did not laugh too much because, after all, Berry was chief of the clan. As he looked at the waning stars in the east, Berry tried to think how it would be possible to prove that they were also present during the day. He was so engrossed in this problem that he did not immediately notice the presence of the Night Comers.

When he did see them, they were already within fifty paces of the ditch that protected the settlement. They stood in a line on the cleared ground, the moonlight giving a cold, sinister glow to their silvered forms. He looked at them and, for a moment or two, was petrified by shock. Then, with one hand already grasping the thong that would sound the alarm bell, he peered at them intently, trying to discern if they were men or monsters.

The night was still, there was no sound. Each of the Night Comers had two shining metal cylinders on his back. Evidently by agreement or command, but with no external sign of either, the Night Comers took slender tubes and pointed them towards the settlement.

For a moment or two, Berry stared at them, hypnotised, frozen. Then he galvanised into action, shaking the thong attached to the bell-striker vigorously. The ringing was loud enough to wake the entire settlement and to hurt Berry's ears. But the Night Comers appeared to take no notice of it. Perhaps they were deaf.

As Berry continued to shake the thong so that the sound of the bell would penetrate the dreams of even the deepest sleepers, three things happened rapidly, one after the other. First, he was gratified to see movement down below as fighting men emerged fully armed from their huts. Second, the tubes held by the Night Comers began to emit long jets of vapour, silvery in the moonlight, which expanded into clouds and drifted over the settlement, slowly becoming invisible as the vapour mixed with the frosty air. Third, the thong which held the bell to the roof-beam of the watch tower was strained to breaking point by Berry's frenzied ringing. Before the bell came crashing down to strike him a glancing blow on the head and an agonising blow on the shoulder, he had a brief glimpse of what was now happening below.

The men who had come out of their huts never had time to take up the defensive positions to which they had previously been assigned. As they ran to their posts, they toppled and lay still. Berry watched with dismay. Then the thong holding up the bell parted. The heavy bell came down, striking him on the head and on the shoulder, taking him into a blessed oblivion that briefly released him from the dreadful knowledge of failure.

Six

HIS SHOULDER HURT ABOMINABLY. His head hurt also, but not so badly as the shoulder. Painfully, Berry got to his feet and peered down from the watch tower.

The only beings in the settlement that moved were the Night Comers. They were dragging unconscious women from the huts by their legs and by their arms. He saw Vron, hauled like meat, like the carcass of a fat deer, to lie with the others. A Night Comer dragged her out of the chief's hut, holding her by an ankle. Her shift was pushed up over her belly, exposing its roundness. The Night Comer did not seem to care. He seemed totally indifferent. He placed her in line with the rest of the women, closed her legs, then went away presumably to seek more females.

Berry was filled with rage and anguish. For a moment or two he was tempted to climb down from the watch tower and fling himself upon these silver monsters who had shamed him for ever by dismissing all his defences, all his precautions, with utter contempt. But reason prevailed. What effect could an injured man have on ten or more of these superhuman creatures who had already defeated the entire Londos people?

Better to observe the creatures, learn how they conducted themselves, discover — if possible — what their weakness was (since every living thing has its weakness as well as its strength) and, perhaps, impart this information at the next fire-talk, before he was invited to embrace the daggers. That he would be required to embrace the daggers, he was sure. He had promised the Londos that the settlement would give greater security from the Night Comers. Yet the defences had been breached as easily as if they were the makeshift defences of a one-night encampment in the forest. The Londos men would remember the promise and would remember that it had been broken. They well knew how to reward the chief who failed them. And it was just, thought Berry bitterly. The tradition was a good one. The chief demanded loyalty from his people, and the people demanded wisdom from their chief. How else could the clan survive?

Well, for the time being, he was still chief of the Londos. Indeed, judging by what was happening below, he was the only member of the clan still in possession of his wits. Therefore it would profit none that he should join the others in their slumbers. Reason dictated that he should observe, remember, and inform the next chief before he embraced the daggers. It was, he felt, a wise decision. Probably his last.

He took comfort from the common belief that the Night Comers never killed. Those clansmen who lay in strange postures with their bows, their swords and their javelins clutched in their hands would rise on the morrow feeling very stupid and aching in every limb. But they would be none the worse for their experience. Within a day, the suppleness would return to their muscles, and they would be men once more.

Berry tried to forget the pain in his head, the dreadful ache in his shoulder, and looked at Vron, supine with her fat pale belly exposed to the grey light of daybreak.

"I will avenge you," he whispered. "If I live, I will avenge you." But the cold, reasoning part of his mind told him that they were just empty words. If he stayed with the Londos, he was already as good as dead. And if he left the Londos, sooner or later he would encounter some other clan who would very likely kill him or, at best, he would be adopted into the clan to take his share of the fighting but not of the women.

Another thought came to him, a good thought. Why should he not trail the Night Comers, follow them back to where they came from, find out the size and strength of their encampment? Then, perhaps, it might be possible to unite the clans at least long enough to mount a massive attack to recover the stolen women. It was a good thought. He had nothing to lose.

Having assembled all the women they could find, or all the women they required, the Night Comers then opened what seemed like pouches on their chests and took out thick metal rods. As Berry watched, they somehow made the rods longer — as long as the height of a man, or a woman. Then they twisted the rods so that each became two rods joined by some kind of thin fabric or skin, broad and transparent. They laid these things upon the ground and each placed the body of an unconscious woman on the fabric between the rods. Then they repeated the process, so that each of the Night Comers dealt with two women. Finally, they brought the rods together over the bodies of the women. When every woman was encased in the transparent fabric, the Night Comers did something that filled Berry with awe. Each of them lifted one woman and tucked her under one arm, then did the same with a second woman and tucked her under the other arm.

The Night Comers stood erect, each carrying the stiff and strangely wrapped bundles of two women. It was a formidable display of strength. No man that Berry had ever known could have held the limp bodies of two women, one under each arm, as the Night Comers did.

Then, still without exchanging any words they marched out of the settlement by the now open and undefended main gate at a walking speed that was nearly twice as fast as that of a man.

Berry stared after them incredulously. Not once did any of them turn and look back. Now he had a problem. What if, when he came down from the watch tower to ground level, there still remained some of the vapour that had rendered the Londos people unconscious? He sniffed the air cautiously and could smell nothing. He would have to take the risk.

Slowly, painfully, he descended the ladder. Whenever he tried to grip it with his left hand, a searing pain went through his shoulder. Several times he nearly fell off; but at last he reached the ground safely. Nothing happened to him. Evidently the vapour had dispersed.

The eastern sky was light now, and the remaining stars were fading rapidly. He hesitated for a moment or two, wondering if he might rouse a few men to go with him. But the time taken to get them sensible might be long enough to cause him to lose track of the Night Comers. He could best serve everyone — Vron, himself, the Londos — by tracking these strange and evil raiders to their encampment or settlement and by learning as much as he could about them. Knowledge was power. This he had always believed.

The Night Comers were already out of sight. But the air was still, and he could hear them marching heavily through the bracken and undergrowth in the woods.

Half-running, half-walking and, after a time, half-fainting, he followed the sound. Sometimes he did not know if he were living or dying, dreaming or waking. Branches whipped at his face and body. He took little notice of them. Sometimes he fell down, and was then glad of the fiery pain in his shoulder. It reminded him that he was still alive. It stopped him from closing his eyes blissfully and sleeping on the frosty earth. It made him stagger to his feet and blunder onwards, following the sound.

Sometimes he caught glimpses of the Night Comers and their grotesque bundles. Then he stayed a while, fearful of discovery. Again he marvelled at these fantastic beings who could each carry two unconscious women and yet travel at such a pace.

Perhaps, indeed, they were gods — or, at least, not mortal. Perhaps they did not feel fatigue as men do. Perhaps they could go on endlessly at this pace, if need be. Perhaps their settlement was at the other end of the world . . . Perhaps . . . Perhaps.

Whatever, as Berry staggered drunkenly on with blood on his face and legs where thorns had torn his flesh, he became convinced that they would surely outlast him. Soon, he knew, he would fall in the forest, this time not minding the pain in his shoulder, never to rise again.

But, strangely, they did not outlast him. The sun was high in the sky when they reached where they were going. Berry had wit enough to realise that. And before he toppled senseless, he saw that to which the Night Comers had brought the stolen women. It was not an encampment or a settlement. It was a great column of metal, smooth, tapering, beautiful, dazzling in the sunlight. It stood in a burned and scorched part of the forest where, evidently, there had been a fire hot enough to reduce tall trees to heaps of white ash.

Berry, his wits gone, all his strength gone, gazed uncomprehendingly at this marvellous thing. So the old ones were right! Indeed there were gods!

He gave a great cry of anguish and fell down. All his

effort had been in vain. For how can a man hope to combat the gods?

The last thing he remembered was a Night Comer bending over him.

And the Night Comer had no face.

Seven

BERRY RETURNED TO CONSCIOUSNESS briefly several times before he at last became fully alert — or as alert as his weakened condition permitted. The first time he opened his eyes, he could not focus properly. He could see only vague shapes and shadows, blue shapes and blue shadows, the quality of blueness unlike anything he had ever experienced. He tried to raise himself, but found that his limbs were either bound or paralysed. He did not know which. Terrified and despairing, he lapsed into unconsciousness once more.

When he next regained his wits, he discovered with relief that his eyes could focus and that he could see things clearly; also that he could move his head. High above him — how high he had no means of knowing — a bluish sphere glowed, somewhat like the moon seen through a heavy mist. The light was dull, but it enabled him to perceive that he was in a kind of circular chamber, the walls of which were dark.

He was not alone. There were many couches — or what looked like couches — supported by metal rods. Stretching his neck painfully, he could see that each couch was suspended above a second couch, which was yet suspended above a third. Lying motionless on each was a woman, her legs, belly and arms bound securely to the couch by broad thongs or strips of fabric. It occurred to him that, since he could move nothing but his head, he too must be bound similarly. He tried to see if Vron

39

was nearby, but could not discern her. The women he could see lay with their mouths slackly open and their eyes closed.

So now he, too, was at the mercy of the Night Comers. His weakened spirit recoiled from terror of the unknown and from the misery of utter failure. Wearily he closed his eyes, hoping that he would die.

He did not die. He dreamed. He dreamed that six men were sitting on his chest, trying to stop him breathing, trying to suffocate him, torturing him to death without the blessed release of a single dagger thrust. He thought hazily that he was at the fire-talk, that he had given an account of his total failure, and that the Londos had judged him unworthy of their weapons.

Painfully, he opened his eyes and saw that this was not so. No one was sitting on his chest, yet each breath was a terrible agony. His head was pressing so hard against the couch that he thought his skull would burst. Somehow, he managed to move his head, though the pain was excruciating and the effort drained him of strength.

The woman on the nearest couch was still unconscious, or seemed to be. But the flesh of her face was distorted, as if gripped and twisted by unseen hands. Her mouth was wide open, the lips drawn away from the teeth. And though she was unconscious, her breasts heaved convulsively; and she groaned and grunted as if a man were taking her against her wish, or as if she were giving birth.

The effort of moving his head proved too much for Berry. He closed his hurting eyes, felt the dreadful weight of the eyelids, and allowed his mind to drift away once more.

When he next awoke, the situation was totally reversed. There was no weight, no pressure. He felt as light as a bird. He tried to move, but his arms and legs were still pinioned. Then he felt that he was falling from a great height. Yet how could he be falling, since he was fastened to a couch? He did not know. But the sensation of falling was terrible and real.

He bit on his tongue to stop himself from crying out. First the choking sensation with the feeling of much weight on his chest; and now the feeling of floating and then falling. He forced himself to glance once more at the women bound upon their couches. There was no movement anywhere. The face of the woman nearest to him was no longer distorted.

Berry thought hard about his predicament. At last, he decided upon a reasonable explanation. I am dying, he told himself. That is plain. I have seen many men die; and I know that sometimes they see things and feel things that others cannot see or feel. Their minds are no longer clear because their minds are dying also. So it is with me; and I must accept it for there is nothing else to do. I regret that I die young; but I can remember many good things that happened in my life, and I know of men who were far less fortunate.

He felt better now that he believed himself to be dying. He was no longer afraid of the falling sensation because he now knew it to be unreal. He stopped biting his tongue and tried to relax. A man should endeavour, at least, to meet his death tranquilly. He coughed a little, and tasted blood in his mouth.

A new thought struck him. If the sensation he had experienced were unreal, why should not this strange place with its foggy blue light and the couches supporting unconscious women also be unreal. Perhaps he was only dreaming as his mind prepared to embark upon the final journey into darkness.

He looked at the nearest woman once more. She *seemed* real — young and with full breasts and full lips.

In happier circumstances, he would have been not unpleased at the prospect of lying with her.

Suppose she *was* real? Suppose it was all real? No, he refused to trouble his aching head any more. It was much better to believe that everything — no matter how substantial it appeared — was only the tormented vision of a dying man.

Suddenly, his resignation was shattered.

There was a bump, and the whole chamber reverberated like a giant bell. Berry's head jerked, the heads of the unconscious women jerked. Then all was still.

After a few moments, there was a sound as of bees buzzing mightily. A section of the dark wall seemed to disappear, and the chamber was filled with bright light. Berry looked at the unconscious women in their couches. Fat women, thin women, ugly women, pretty women. It was absurd that all these could be imagined in such detail by a weak and dying mind.

Night Comers walked through the opening that had been created in the wall. Methodically, they began to loose the fastenings that bound the women to their couches. Methodically, they began to strip the women of their clothes.

Berry was filled with a sense of rage. He looked at the slack, naked bodies in the chamber; and anger gave him strength. When one of the Night Comers loosed his bonds, he began to strike it feebly with his good arm on its faceless metal head.

The Night Comer did not seem alarmed or angry. He restrained Berry gently, as one might restrain a child. Though he had no lips, he uttered words that sounded familiar but were yet beyond understanding. Berry lay on his couch, impotent and with rage in his heart, held firmly but gently by one metallic hand while the Night Comer used a small, shining instrument to cut away his sheepskin jacket. He was lifted gently while the remnants of clothing were taken from his body. Then he, too, lay as naked as the women. The fastenings were placed around him once more, so that he was unable to move. He strained against them and only succeeded in hurting his shoulder. Then he lay back gasping, and contented himself with trying to see what was happening.

Two or three Night Comers were collecting all the sad remnants of doe-skin and sheep-skin and woven cloth. These were placed in transparent sacks. When each sack was full, it was sealed and taken away through the opening whence the bright light came.

Soon all the clothing had gone. All that remained in the chamber was one naked man and many naked women — perhaps thirty or forty bodies, each bound securely once more to its couch.

They were skinning us, thought Berry crazily, as we would skin rabbits. What manner of creatures are they that can treat human beings thus?

When the clothing had gone, the Night Comers began to loosen each block of three couches from whatever had fastened them to the floor of the chamber. Straining his neck, so that his shoulder hurt most abominably, Berry was able to see that the rods supporting the couches each had small wheels at the base. As the couches were loosened, they were wheeled through the bright opening.

Presently the three couches of which Berry occupied the topmost were made loose and removed from the chamber. The light outside the chamber was so bright that Berry was dazzled for a few moments. When his eyes had adjusted, he saw that he was being taken down a long passage. Finally his block of couches came to rest in a well-lit circular chamber to which the other couches had been brought. The wall of the chamber was transparent but misted as by drops of moisture. He thought he saw people — human beings — on the other side of the wall. But he could have been mistaken.

When all the couches had been brought to the chamber, the Night Comers left it, closing the opening behind them.

For a while, nothing happened.

Berry lay on his couch, surrounded by unconscious women, and wondered if there was now about to be some dreadful ritual sacrifice. It was a crazy thought. It occurred to him that, because of his own foolishness, he had been brought along with these poor women to the land of unreason. Formerly, he had supposed that the Night Comers required women for breeding. But how could a creature covered in silvery metal lie with a woman and get a child?

In the land of unreason, the place where anything was possible, might not the Night Comers require the lives of human females to propitiate whatever gods they believed in? Alternatively, perhaps they hunted women as the clans hunted deer. Perhaps they regarded women as a source of food. But why not men also? Berry's head ached, his shoulder ached, his whole body ached. He was weak, and he knew he was not thinking sensibly.

Suddenly he was aware of a pain in his ears. It was a strange, agonising pain — as if something inside his head were trying to force a way out. His skin began to tingle, and his eyes felt as if they would burst out of their sockets. He tried to breathe; but it was as if the very air were being sucked out of his lungs. There was a great roaring in his head and his body felt as if it were being torn apart. He tried to scream; but he had no voice. Before he lost his wits, he glimpsed the naked women jerking spasmodically against their bonds, as he was. Then bright lights exploded in his head and brought merciful oblivion.

He thought he had died, but he was wrong. Or, if he had died, then he was now restored to painful life by thin jets of white fluid that splashed forcefully all over his body, face, eyes, mouth. He swallowed some as his lungs gulped air thankfully once more. The taste was bitter. He coughed convulsively. Perhaps the fluid was poisonous. He hoped it was. He wanted the madness to end. He had had more than enough of it.

There were so many jets of fluid hitting his body, creating a whitish mist, that he could hardly see the women around him. The nearest one, bombarded as he was by a myriad jets, lay passive with her eyes closed while rivulets of the fluid dripped from her breasts like unwanted milk. Berry hoped that the others also remained unaware of what was happening.

Presently, the jets stopped. Clouds of vapour rolled like fog through the chamber and subsided slowly. One woman at least had returned to consciousness. He heard a thin scream that tailed off into a wail, followed by agonised sobbing.

Suddenly, he felt very cold and began to shiver. He could not stop the shivering. Restrained as he was by bonds, he shook so much that he thought he would shake himself apart. He could feel ice crystals on his flesh. The sensation was horrible.

He saw snow flakes in the air. Snow flakes forming and drifting down on the bodies of the helpless women. He blinked, and his eyelids froze together. He tried to open them; but he had no strength left. He could only lie there and feel the dreadful coldness eating into his body.

Now, I must surely die, he thought with relief.

He was wrong.

The snow melted rapidly, his eyelids became unfrozen. A blast of warm air brought life to his numbed flesh.

Rapidly, the air became warmer, and warmer and warmer. Hot. Unbearably hot.

He started to sweat. He gasped, breathing convulsively. The hot air seared his lungs. Each breath was an agony.

He saw visions.

Vron approached him. She was misshapen, grotesque. Her breasts were larger than any breasts he had ever seen. Her buttocks, too, were enormous — like the rump of a cow. She danced. Her dance was wild, immodest, inviting. He strained to reach her, but he could not move.

A Night Comer appeared. He had silver cylinders on his back and carried a silver tube in his hand. He danced with Vron. Presently, he pointed the silver tube towards her belly. A jet of vapour came from it. Vron opened her legs and sucked the vapour into her womb. There was a mad look on her face, a look of mindless ecstasy.

The Night Comer disappeared. Vron crouched in the birth position. She laboured, grunting and sweating. Then she brought forth a tiny, silver creature from between her legs. It made no sound, but crawled up her body to take milk from one of the massive breasts. Another creature emerged. It, too, found the other breast. Vron still squatted in the birth position, her lips parted, her tongue protruding, her eyes vacant, while the little silver creatures clung to her breasts, sucking the milk of life.

Berry tried to call to Vron, tried to tell her to stop suckling demons. But his shout was no more than an exhausted sigh. He was too weak to do anything.

The vision dissolved.

He was so painfully hot that he knew he must be cooking—like a wild pig on a spit over a slow fire. He wondered vaguely how the flesh of man would taste. Would it be like pig's flesh or like venison or like beef? An interesting problem.

46

The cooking stopped abruptly. Jets of fluid played over his body once more, cool, healing, invigorating. He tasted the fluid in his parched mouth. It was wonderful. It tasted like cold spring water.

A Night Comer lifted his head, said something that he did not understand, presented a cup to his lips. Berry drank greedily, not caring what was in the cup.

It tasted sweet, it tasted strong, it tasted wonderful. It annihilated pain and memory. It brought instant oblivion.

Eight

HE WOKE WITH THE knowledge that voices in his head had been talking for a long time. At first he had not been able to understand what they were saying; but now he knew exactly what they were saying, though the words were in a different tongue than his own. The voices had told him that he was safe and that he would not be hurt. Strangely, he believed them — perhaps because they had repeated the message so many times.

He felt very drowsy, very comfortable. It was with great difficulty that he managed to keep his eyes open. He saw that he was no longer naked. He was wearing some kind of tunic, warm, pleasing to touch. He was alone, lying on a couch in a small dimly-lit chamber. His shoulder no longer hurt. He found he could move his arms and legs freely. But he did not want to. It was too much effort. He felt very tired. Tired and comfortable.

He scratched his ear, and discovered that something like a small round pebble was lodged in it. He yawned and tried to take the pebble out. It was so smooth that he could not get a grip on it. Well, that did not matter. It was not hurting him. It felt quite pleasant, really. Perhaps he would take it out when he was less tired.

The voices in his head told him to rest, that he had nothing to fear. They sounded like very wise voices. He was sure they spoke the truth. He was mildly surprised that he could understand them so easily, though the tongue was strange. He took their advice. He began to doze once more.

The voices continued to talk, sometimes to whisper. He did not mind. They were very friendly voices. Sometimes he listened to them, sometimes not.

Presently, the voices stopped. He waited for them to return, to speak to him again. But they did not. Somehow, he was not surprised.

He felt wide awake and fully refreshed. His body was strong, and there was no sign of injury on his shoulder. He remembered about the smooth pebble in his ear, and tried to get it out. But it was not there. Perhaps he had dreamed that it was there. No matter. He felt good.

He remembered much. He remembered about the Night Comers and the high shining column in a scorched part of the forest. He remembered how the women had been stripped of their clothes. He remembered the jets of fluid, the heat and the cold, and being unable to breathe. He remembered the terrible sensation of falling.

But none of it seemed to matter any more. It was as if it belonged to another world, another life.

Perhaps he was dead. If so, this life after death seemed quite pleasant. Perhaps he was in the place the old ones called heaven. If so, it was not a bad place. Perhaps he would meet Oris here — that would be a bad encounter. There would surely be matters that Oris wished to discuss further. Or perhaps he would meet Riel the singer, the brother of Vron. That would be a better encounter. But not a much better encounter, perhaps. What if Riel demanded to know how Berry had cared for his sister? Now that might be an embarrassment. A clansman had the right to mortal combat with anyone, including his chief, if that person had been guilty of betraying, injuring or failing to protect a member of his family.

Did I fail to protect Vron? Berry asked himself.

The answer was yes. There were excuses, perhaps. But the answer was yes. Berry had failed to protect her against the Night Comers.

Still, he reasoned, if I am dead and in heaven, surely I cannot die twice. If I meet Riel, I will explain to him what has happened. He will know that no man can be expected to stand against the Night Comers.

As he thought these thoughts, a Night Comer entered the chamber. He carried a cup.

"Drink this, master," he said. He had no face, no eyes, no mouth. Yet the words were clear. Nor were they in the language of the clans. Yet Berry understood them fully.

He took the cup. "What is this you now give me?" The liquid was warm and golden.

"You wish to know the chemical formula, master?"

Berry recognised the words 'chemical formula' and wondered why he should recognise them when they had no meaning for him. He, too, spoke in the strange tongue that was strangely familiar. "I wish to know if this drink will poison me or render me helpless, that is all, Night Comer. You are my enemy and you have brought me close to death — if, indeed, I am not already dead and in the world where the dead are supposed to dwell — therefore, I seek to know the nature of this cup. I know you may or may not choose to speak the truth, but that is a problem I must use my wits on."

"Master, the drink is beneficial. It will give you strength. It will eliminate any discomfort, it will banish fear. With regret and apology, I must correct your statement. I am not your enemy and I have not brought you close to death. Also, I am programmed to speak the truth."

"What if I choose not to take this drink?"

"I am not empowered to compel you, master."

Now here was something Berry could test. He tilted the

50

cup and slowly poured its contents on the floor. The Night Comer made no move to stop him.

"It is regretted that you did not drink. The liquid was formulated for the assistance of human beings under stress conditions."

Berry was amazed. He gazed at the face that was no face, that was but a smooth silver mask with a transparent strip where on a man there would have been eyes; and he tried to discern some change of expression. But there was none because the mask was of metal. A man might betray his feelings by his face. But not a Night Comer. Yet what if a man lurked inside the metal skin? Would he not have feelings?

"You are not angry because I did not drink from the cup you brought?"

"No, master. I cannot be angry." The voice was even. "Perhaps you would like to re-evaluate. Shall I bring another dose of trank?"

Berry did not understand the meaning of the words; but he did understand that the Night Comer had not been provoked by his action.

Recklessly, he decided to experiment further. He spat on the creature's mask. If he had spit in the face of a clansman, it would have resulted in a duel to the death. He tensed himself, waiting for the metal hands to reach out, preparing to spring.

But the Night Comer did nothing. The spittle dripped down his mask He did not even attempt to wipe it away.

"Permit me, master, to enquire why you ejected saliva from your mouth? Are you unwell?"

Berry gazed uncomprehendingly at the creature. "I spit upon you, yet you do not take offence."

"I am not empowered to take offence."

Berry began to laugh. It was, he knew, hysterical laughter — such noises as a woman might make when she had suffered greatly. So now, in his weakness of spirit, he had become as a woman. It was humiliating. With an effort, he managed to stop the laughter. He felt tears running down his face, and was ashamed.

At last he was able to speak calmly. "You bind me and torture me. You place great weights upon my chest then you cause me to have the terrible sensation of falling. You draw the breath from my body, you freeze me then half-cook me, and impose such suffering as is hardly to be borne. Then you call me master, concern yourself with my well-being and do nothing when I spit upon you. What manner of people are you Night Comers? Are you gods or devils, or madmen lurking behind silver armour?"

"Master, I am a computer-controlled robot and I must fulfil my programme. The discomfort you experienced is regrettable. It was caused by the transference from Earth to orbit and by the standard decontamination procedure. Because of a fault in the programme, which is concerned basically with the acquisition of human females, erroneous data about your condition was fed back to control. There are those who will orient you better than I can. I am empowered to escort you to them. Are you able to walk? If so, will you come voluntarily?"

Berry's head was spinning. He did not understand the term 'robot'. He did not understand what was meant by computer-control. But he remembered the voices in his head that told him he had nothing to fear. Strangely, he still believed them.

"What if I do not choose to come voluntarily?"

"Then, master, I would have to transport you. I would endeavour to cause minimal discomfort."

Berry had little doubt that the Night Comer could take him forcibly with small apparent effort.

"Those to whom you are commanded to take me — are they such as you?"

52

"No, master. They are human beings."

"Then I will walk," said Berry. "I am of a mind to gaze upon the faces of men who can control such creatures as you."

He was led out of the chamber down a long corridor to a hall that seemed to be bathed in sunlight. There were several people in the hall. One of them sat on a great chair that glittered with the brilliance of polished metal and crystal.

The rest stood close by him and gazed at Berry with expressions of amusement and curiosity. Berry was quick to notice that one or two of the women eyed him favourably. It raised his spirits.

The Night Comer who had brought him to the hall retreated. Berry was left standing alone. The man on the great chair inspected him carefully.

"Welcome to Heaven," he said. "The acquisition programme is entirely for females; but the occasional enterprising male does not displease us."

Nine

ONE THING WAS CERTAIN, thought Berry, striving to keep his wits about him, Heaven was not the abode of the dead. For these people were demonstrably much alive. Their flesh was like his flesh. Some of the men — who were almost all taller than he — wore nothing but kilts, such as the northern clans wore, but of fine fabric having the sheen of metals, of gold and silver and bright steel. And many of the women wore flowing garments that exposed their breasts, apparently not caring if anyone should gaze upon them with desire.

"Well, fellow," said the man on the great chair, "have the teaching machines not programmed you to understand our language?" He smiled. "Or is your tongue paralysed by the wonders you now see?"

"Are you the chief of this clan?" demanded Berry, looking — he hoped — more calm than he felt.

His question occasioned some laughter. He gazed about him apprehensively, afraid that in some way he did not understand he was making a fool of himself.

"I am Regis Le Gwyn, elected Controller of Heaven Seven. But, in your terms of reference, I am chief of this clan. What is your name, fellow? And how did you come to involve yourself in the collection programme?"

"I know nothing of your collection programme, Regis Le Gwyn. I know only that the Night Comers — your warriors, I think — attacked my settlement and took many women, among them one who is mine. My name is Berry.

I am chief of the Londos. You have done me an injury.
I demand an accounting." Berry took a deep breath.
"Therefore I challenge you to mortal combat."

Regis Le Gwyn was vastly amused. "You are called
Berry, nothing but Berry?"

"That is my name."

"It is not much of a name. Here we have better ones
for our dogs."

"It is the name of the man who will kill you," said
Berry ferociously. "Now have done with words, and let
us choose weapons. Also, chief, let your clan see that the
combat is fair."

Again there was much amusement. Berry was dis-
concerted, not knowing what to make of these people.
Here he was, chief of a clan, demanding the ancient
right of combat to the death with the chief of those who
had attacked the Londos. And all these people could do
was laugh. He gazed about him in bewilderment.

"Berry, listen to me carefully," said Regis Le Gwyn.
"You are a dirt savage, an animal, and stupid as all dirt
savages are. You will not fight with me — though if you
desire to shed blood there may be opportunities. Instead,
you will learn about this world to which you have been
brought. You will learn that we of Heaven Seven are your
superiors, as much above you as you are above the wild
pigs you hunt in your dirtside forest. Because if you do
not learn to please us, your body will be dismantled.
Your eyes — if they are good — will be taken from your
head and used to give sight to another. Your heart, your
lungs and your kidneys, if they are healthy, will also
be deposited in the organ bank against our needs. The
rest of you — your bones, your flesh and your brain, such
as it is — will be processed to fertilise our gardens, to
cause roses to bloom beautifully and peaches to become

succulent. Remember all this, Nothing-but-Berry. For you it is the difference between life and death."

With a great cry of rage, Berry tensed himself to spring. "Stand, if you are a man!" he roared. "Else I will choke the life out of you where you sit!"

Regis Le Gwyn took something from his robe. It was small, shiny, metallic. He pointed it at Berry. "Receive your first lesson, savage."

A narrow beam of radiance, thin as a bone needle, came from the small metallic thing and struck Berry on his leg. Instantly, he fell to the floor, writhing in pain. There was a smell of burning flesh. He looked at his leg and saw, disbelievingly, a small black hole, a scorched circle of skin with smoke and steam still rising from it. He willed himself not to cry out with the pain, not to shame himself before his enemy. He tried to stand, and could not. The effort brought a mist to his eyes, but he was determined not to lose his senses.

He heard the calm voice of Regis Le Gwyn. "Remove this savage. Heal his wound. Let him be instructed by one of his own kind in words that he will understand. Better still, let him have the use of a third-pregnancy dirt female. They may derive some consolation from each other before she is put down."

Again there was laughter. Berry tried vainly to use his eyes; but the mist had become as a thick fog, and he felt like a blind man. He had not lost his senses, though. And that was something.

"Controller, it shall be as you instruct. Computer control informs that there are nineteen third-pregnancy females now available."

Berry recognised the voice as that of one of the Night Comers. They all had the same kind of voice, clear and unemotional. Inhuman.

"Let him have the youngest, then," said Regis Le

Gwyn. "He is, he says, a clan chief. So perhaps we should accord him reasonable hospitality."

Berry heard the humiliating laughter once more. Then he was picked up effortlessly by the Night Comer and taken away. He could not see, but he knew that he was being carried like a child. With a last surge of strength, he made his hand into a fist and struck where he thought the Night Comer's head would be.

He groaned in anguish, knowing that he had broken two or three finger bones.

"I am sorry, master," said the Night Comer. "It is advisable for you to relax. Your injuries will be attended to by skilled robots. There is no irreparable damage."

Berry fainted.

Ten

BERRY FOUND HIMSELF IN a chamber more spacious and more comfortable than the one he had recently occupied. It contained a couch broad enough for two people to lie upon and many things whose purpose he did not yet understand. In one of the walls there was a large hole which admitted bright light through some crystal substance. There was also a woman in the chamber. She had white hair, but a young face. And, though her clothing was strange, Berry recognised her as a clanswoman. She had the look of a Manches woman. The Manches people were noted for the softness and paleness of their skins.

"My name is Tala," she said in the tongue of the clans. "You have slept a long time. I tried to be quiet so that I would not wake you before you were ready."

Now Berry was sure she was a Manches woman. Her accent betrayed her. He raised himself from the couch and rested on an elbow. He looked at the leg that had been wounded. There was no trace of injury, no scar. Though the skin where there should have been a scar felt strangely insensitive. He flexed the fingers of the hand with which he had struck the Night Comer. They worked perfectly. There was no pain. Evidently the bones had not been broken. Or, if they had, they had been mended most skilfully.

"Tala, I am Berry, chief of the Londos." He grimaced. "Well, I was once chief of the Londos ... You know my people?"

"I have heard of them. They are not a warlike clan. That is all I know."

"Not warlike," said Berry. "But also not weak. We know how to fight when we must."

Tala gave a bitter laugh. "You could not prevent the Night Comers from taking your women, could you?"

"Who can?" said Berry. "We do not understand their ways or their skills."

Suddenly, Tala was crying.

"I have borne three babies," she sobbed. "My time is short, and I am much afraid."

Berry was perplexed. "Hush, woman," he said gently. "Weeping achieves little. I do not understand your misery. Many women bear three babies — ay, and more. It is a woman's task to bring forth babies. What of that? The first one is the hardest, so they say."

"They were not my babies," sobbed Tala. "Nor were they begot by men of Earth. No one has lain with me, yet I have given birth three times." She sniffed, trying to control her weeping. "Forgive me, Berry. I did not mean to plague you with my misery. I was sent here to instruct you, not to add to your troubles."

Berry scratched his head. "If no man has lain with you, how could you bring forth babies?"

"The Lords of Heaven had them put in my belly while I slept. That is the truth. They do not lie with dirt women, or only rarely. They have strange instruments, and much magic, whereby they can plant the seed of a child in the womb of a woman without her knowing. So it was with me. I have given them three sons. When a woman has given birth three times, the Lords of Heaven consider her spent. She is taken from the seminary and is not seen again. Some say that such women are returned Dirtside, but others say they are killed, that the Lords of

Heaven make use of their bodies to grow flowers. That is why I am afraid."

Berry's mind was in a whirl. "What is Dirtside?" he said. "What is this talk of dirt women and dirt men? The chief of this place called me a dirt savage. I know that it is an insult, but I do not understand its meaning."

Tala wiped her eyes, tried to smile. "Berry, you have much to learn. The world in which we lived before the Night Comers took us is called Dirtside by the Lords of Heaven. We call it Earth, but they call it Dirtside. Also, this place, this Heaven Seven, they sometimes call Heavenside. I do not fully understand why this should be so. But it is their pleasure. Though they look like us, they are a strange and powerful people. We dirtside folk cannot hope to get the better of them. So we have to submit to their will and bear what we must."

"All that will have to be changed," said Berry, sounding more confident than he felt. "Tell me, woman, where is this Heavenside? If I can escape, how long will it take me to march back to my own people?"

Tala gave him a pitying smile. "You will never march back to your own people, Berry. There is no escape. Heavenside is an island in the sky."

"An island in the sky?" Berry felt that she must be lying, though she did not look like one who was lying. "I have looked up at the sky, Tala, many times in the day and in the night. I have seen no island. I have seen only the sun, moon and the stars. Therefore how can this be?"

"I speak truly. Heavenside is so far away from Dirtside that it does not look like an island. But perhaps you have seen it and not known . . . Have you seen the Wanderer?"

"Who with good eyes has not seen it?" retorted Berry. "It is the largest star in the sky, if not the brightest. It passes smoothly through the darkness, sometimes seeming to pass through the moon itself. Though, as any reasonable man knows, that cannot be."

"The Wanderer is Heaven Seven," said Tala. "It is that place wherein we now live and must die."

Berry became angry. He took her wrist, held it tightly. "Woman, do not take me for a fool. Do not mock my ignorance. Tell me the truth, or I will give you good cause for weeping."

"Hurt me," she said wearily. "It will add little to your manhood, I think." She shrugged. "It matters not to me. Having borne my three, I have but a short time left. If death is to be my lot, they say the Lords of Heaven are merciful, and there will be no pain."

Berry's perplexity grew. "What is all this talk of birth and death?" He got up abruptly from the couch on which he had been sitting with Tala and, stretching his legs, was surprised to find that his feet briefly left the floor. He looked down at them in amazement. Then, experimentally, he made a little jump. He rose higher than he had intended and seemed to fall more slowly than he should have done. He felt strangely light. Perhaps it was a result of his recent injury. "Am I ill, woman? My muscles feel stronger than they should be. Yet there seems to be little substance to my body."

Tala said, surprisingly and in the alien tongue: "Rest easy, Berry. Your mass has not changed. You are in a field of synthetic gravity. That is all."

Berry passed a hand over his forehead. "I am sorry if I was rough. It seems I have much to learn. I know the words you use, but I do not understand their meaning."

"There are no such words in the language of the clans. That is why I must speak to you heavenwise."

"Then do so. I will try to be patient. I will try to understand . . . Three births, you said. And now you are afraid of death. You have been here — you have been in

Heavenside — a long time, Tala. Tell me your story. My head aches with many mysteries. Help me to make sense of this world. That is all I ask."

"I will do my best. Believe only that I speak the truth. Though we are of different clans, we are dirtside people among strangers, powerful strangers. We must help each other."

"I believe that, and I believe that you will speak the truth."

"Then seal the bargain with your mouth against mine, with your body against mine, with your hand on my breast."

"At a time like this?"

"We are dirtside savages, Berry, in the power of the Lords of Heaven. Time runs short for both of us, I think. Let us take pleasure while we may."

Berry held her close and laid her upon the couch. Tala moaned with pleasure. As he caressed her, Berry thought: There will be a time for understanding. This woman needs a man badly. Afterwards she will be grateful. Afterwards, she will tell me all I need to know.

Eleven

TALA'S STORY WAS STRANGE — stranger than the night-mares mumbled crazily at the mid-summer fire-talk, when almost all the clans people, even the children, were drunk on the boiled juices of the five friendly mushrooms.

She had been brought Heavenside in much the same way that the women of the Londos — and Berry himself — had been brought. She, too, had found that she could understand the Heavenside language that was different from, but not greatly different from, the language of the clans.

When she had become sensible, and no longer screamed at the approach of a Night Comer or crouched like an animal at bay before her captors, she was given to the Lady Sontag, a woman admired greatly by many of the Lords and Ladies of Heaven because she fashioned objects in stone and wood that were much prized.

The Lady Sontag, Tala explained, was beautiful and — by Heavenside standards — kind. She lay with most men who asked her and, though she was envied by women of lesser renown, she cultivated their friendship. Also she was kind to her slaves, of whom Tala had been the third and the youngest in her time of serving.

Though the Lady Sontag was, by dirtside reckoning, more than one hundred and seventy years old, and though she had lain with many men, no child had ever been born of her womb. Yet nineteen of her children had been brought forth from the wombs of successive slaves.

63

Of those children, but three had survived to maturity. The rest had succumbed to strange diseases.

Berry asked how the child of one woman could be brought forth from the body of another. Tala did not properly know. She knew only that she had given birth to three babies, each of whom the Lady Sontag had claimed as her own. Two of these had died early. One still lived. Though, from what the Lady Sontag said, there was little hope that the survivor would endure long. Such was the case with many babies born in Heaven. Thus, because of the rule of three, many dirtside women were needed so that the Ladies might enjoy watching at least a few of their children reach manhood and womanhood, and so that the Heavenside people might continue to exist.

Berry wondered why the women of this place did not bear their own children. It seemed to him that if they did this naturally, as the women of Earth did, there might not be so much death among the young. But, according to Tala, the act of childbirth was considered to be very dangerous for Heavenside women. In the past, they had endeavoured to carry their babies in their bellies; but frequently many of the babies had been brought forth long before they were fully formed. And of those who did last their full season, some had no arms or legs, or were blind, some perished upon being born; and often the mothers died also. Further, it was known that the Ladies of Heaven could only live to a great age, still enjoying youth and beauty, if they were not subjected to the strain of carrying and bearing young. A Heavenside woman, if she were lucky enough to bear a normal child and survive the ordeal, thereafter aged rapidly. Men would no longer look upon her with favour. In a few years, she became old and withered as a dirtside woman who had seen fifty or more summers.

As Tala talked, Berry's overworked mind tried to make

some sense of the world and the society into which he had been thrust. Heaven Seven, he learned, did not contain only Lords and Ladies and the strange beings he knew as the Night Comers. Nor were its people divided into clans — at least, not into clans that he would have recognised as such. The Lords and Ladies, he discovered, were called ristos and were almost the smallest group in this strange world that evidently floated between Earth and the stars. The smallest group of all was a kind of brotherhood/ sisterhood called the teknos. Though small in numbers, and though the rules of their group forbade the men to lie with women, or the women to lie with men, the teknos were very powerful. It was they who served the computers, the magical instruments which controlled the actions of the robots, known to Berry as the Night Comers. The chief of the teknos was the Programmer, and his power was second only to the Controller, whom Berry had already painfully encountered.

Below the ristos and teknos, there were the nilskils. They had no chief. But they were the largest clan; and they obeyed without question the instructions of their superiors. They were ambitious yet servile, because it was from their group that the ristos and teknos were drawn, depending on their eye cues, tee cues and pee cues.

Tala did not fully understand what eye cue was. Nor was she any wiser about the nature of a tee cue or a pee cue. She only knew that they were important, determining whether a nilskil should prosper or not. The Lady Sontag, who had treated Tala more as a friend than a slave, had endeavoured to explain about intelligence quotients, talent quotients and performance quotients. But Tala had remained none the wiser. She knew that these words were concerned with skill and quickness of wit, and that was all. How could she be expected to understand

65

more? She was only a dirtside savage whose number had come up. The dreaded number three.

When the tekno inspector came to remove her from the Lady Sontag's home, both Tala and Sontag cried. It was to no avail. The ordinance of the Programmer could not be denied, even by a risto. However, the Lady Sontag went so far as to appeal to the Controller, the only man in Heaven who outranked the Programmer and could — theoretically — countermand his decree. The Lady Sontag petitioned that Tala be accorded the status of a nilskil which, at least, would give her the privileges of residence. There were precedents. Over the centuries, a few dirtside women had been elevated to nilskils at the request of various Lords who found them attractive to lie with. But, in each case, the request had only been granted for a woman who had borne three unblemished babies. Which was not the case with Tala. Therefore, the petition was denied.

So Tala's last Heavenside task was to instruct Berry in the ways of this strange world. After that, she knew not what.

Berry was sorry for her. He knew of no woman who had been returned to her clan by the Night Comers, or the robots, as they were called in this place. Therefore, he assumed that, when the Lords of Heaven had no further use for the dirtside women their robots obtained, those women would be killed. It seemed reasonable. But he did not tell Tala that it seemed reasonable. He did not wish to deprive her of hope — if, indeed, she had any left.

But while she lived, while they were allowed to remain together, he wished to obtain as much knowledge from her as was possible.

"This world, Heaven Seven, has it always been passing through our sky? If not, where has it come from? Will it ever go away? Will it ever leave our people alone?"

Tala smiled. "Berry, you must trust me. I have learned much from the Lady Sontag and others. It may be that they were lying, that they all lie to dirtside people. But I do not think so . . . They say that long ago on Earth, there was a race with great powers, magical powers."

"The people who made the hot spots?"

"Just so. The time in which they lived was called the atomic age. I do not understand this word atomic. But I have been told that atomic energy — whatever that is — yielded heat a thousand times more powerful than the hottest fire, perhaps as hot even as the sun itself. The atomic people learned to use this energy in two terrible ways. They learned to use it to drive great machines and to destroy each other. But before they destroyed each other and, in doing so, made the hot spots, they used their atomic energy to lift great vessels from the face of the Earth. Some of these vessels voyaged to the moon and beyond. Some were simply placed in orbit."

"In orbit? What does this mean?"

"It means that the vessels were steered so that they would voyage endlessly round the Earth at a great distance. I have been told that certain wise men, knowing that this atomic energy would eventually destroy their own people, made plans to use these vessels to build islands in the sky, so that their race would not entirely perish. Heaven One was the first of these islands. It was something that the Lady Sontag calls a space laboratory. The important thing was that men and women could live upon it. They could grow their own food, not depending upon the flesh or fruits of Earth to sustain them.

"As time passed, and before the atomic people began to destroy each other, they constructed many of these islands, some in the same orbit, some in different orbits, closer to Earth or farther away from it. For a while, there were many small islands in the sky. Some of them

67

were so small that they had to be supplied with food and even air from Earth. Others, only a few, were large enough to develop a total recycling system."

Berry scratched his head, trying to comprehend. "This total recycling system — it is a machine to make air and food?"

Tala shrugged. "Forgive me, Berry, if I do not explain these matters clearly. My own understanding is not good." She thought for a moment or two. "What happens when a man or an animal dies in the forest and is left there? What happens when dead leaves fall, when anything dies and returns to the earth which gave it life?"

"It rots," said Berry. "The flesh begins to stink. The flies attack it, the creatures of the forest attack it. What is left — even bones — are destroyed by time. The substance sinks into the ground, washed by the rains, whether it be animal or plant, to be consumed by the earth which gave it sustenance."

"And then?"

Again Berry scratched his head. "Why then the earth brings forth new life which, in turn, perishes ... What has this to do with what you call a total recycling system?"

"Berry, as I understand the Lady Sontag and others, this is what is meant by a total recycling system. The living perish and from their substance new life is created." She faltered. "I fear that I, too, may be recycled now that my usefulness is at an end. But I will try not to dwell upon it because there is nothing that you or I can do to prevent it ... I was telling you how the islands in the sky came to be formed. Heaven One, as I said, was the first. But there were many others, placed in orbit by different clans of the atomic people. Some had recycling systems, some had not. When the atomic wars began, the people on those islands which could not recycle

68

perished as their supplies failed and vessels did not rise from the Earth to renew them. It was then that Heaven Two was created. The teknos of Heaven One found a way of taking the dead islands out of near orbits and joining them to Heaven One. As time passed, their skills became better, their strength greater. Heaven Two was controlled by the Usa people; but the Rusks, the Chines and the Uros also had islands which could recycle. First, the Usa people made peace with the Uros and brought their two islands together. That was Heaven Three. It became the most powerful island. While the Rusks and the Chines were trying to make war — which is difficult if you are in different orbits — Heaven Three became strong. Eventually, its teknos found a way of lifting Heaven Three into the Rusk orbit. The Rusk island was joined to make Heaven Four. Later, Heaven Four lifted yet again to join with the Chine island. That was Heaven Five. Heaven Six was created when the teknos brought all the dead islands up into the new orbit. The material thus gained by Heaven Six enabled its teknos to create new Earth-to-orbit vessels. And so the robots — the Night Comers — were able to descend to Earth and bring back the materials and the women needed to create Heaven Seven . . . That is the story. I have told it badly, I fear. But I am only a dirtside woman, and do not understand much of these things."

Berry stroked her hair gently. "Tala, you have spoken well. I have tried hard to understand all that you have said. But my mind is much confused, though I believe you speak of what you know . . . It seems there will be much difficulty in escaping from this island in the sky. We shall need to steal one of those Earth-to-orbit vessels of which you spoke and we shall need to learn how to control it. Yes, there will be much difficulty. I must think hard."

Tala began to laugh. "Much difficulty! Berry, it is impossible. These people are as far beyond us as we are beyond the creatures of the forest. They and their machines are all-powerful. There is nothing we can do."

"Unless they kill me," said Berry stubbornly, "I will find a way to get back to Earth. This I swear."

Twelve

BERRY AND TALA WERE kept in the chamber for three Heavenside days. This he knew because the light which came through the circular piece of crystal set in the wall — which Tala called a window — waxed and waned regularly. At certain times, a section of the wall opened noiselessly to admit a robot bearing food. The second time this happened, Berry thought to attack the robot and escape. Still holding the tray of food, the robot used his free arm to restrain Berry. With amazing speed, mechanical fingers gripped the fist that had been aimed at the robot's head and held it firmly, effortlessly.

"Master, I have no instructions to let you pass. Please do not hurt yourself uselessly."

Holding Berry's fist in an unbreakable grip, the robot propelled him back into the chamber as if it were dealing with a rebellious child.

Berry sat on the couch, ashamed, and nursed his aching hand.

"You see," said Tala. "Courage is not enough. There is nothing to be done."

When the robot had gone and the opening in the wall had closed, Berry tried for the tenth time to peer through the window. And for the tenth time failed to discern anything outside. The window admitted light, but he could not see clearly through it.

The food was good. Some of it was meat, recognisable as such but cooked in a way that gave it subtle flavour.

Some was the seed of plants or the leaves, and some was a white, pleasant-tasting substance which Tala called tatos.

Under Tala's instruction, he learned to use the wash basin and the lavatory, and learned also how to switch on the light when the light coming through the window failed. At dusk, Tala would sing for Berry. She would sing some of the old clan songs — not the battle chants or any of the songs that recorded memorable victories because, after all, they were of different clans. Instead, she sang sadly and beautifully the dirges, the love songs that were common to all the clans. Afterwards they would lie together, holding each other very close, feeling sometimes — so Berry thought — like small, frightened children not yet old enough or wise enough to understand much of the world about them.

They did not sleep much during the night. Tala had a sense of doom, believing that her life was approaching its end, cherishing and savouring every moment of continued existence. She needed to be consoled greatly. Berry did his best. But even when she moaned and grunted with the pleasure of his body upon hers and of his seed flowing into her womb, he still felt the immense sadness in her, the foreboding of death. Sometimes, when he was taking her, when she was giving herself to him, he thought of Vron. Then he would try desperately to put Vron out of his mind. He could not know what was happening to her, and very likely he would never see her again.

Morning would find Tala and Berry exhausted, not only by the night's intimacy but by their separate nightmares which followed it. Yet he was not too tired to learn as much as Tala could tell him of this island in the sky which had now become his prison. He discovered that Heaven Seven was divided into three parts called Citizone, Faczone and Parkzone.

Citizone was where the ristos and the nilskils lived. Citizone contained houses, apartment blocks, theatres, restaurants, bars, baths. Berry knew the words — Tala could only talk about Heavenside things in the Heavenside tongue — but he did not understand them, his experience being only of the things of Earth. Tala did her best to explain about houses, theatres and the rest; and Berry did his best to comprehend. But such wonders made his mind reel.

Faczone, so Tala said, was a place of mysteries and magic, where the teknos reigned supreme, served by their robots, their computers and their autofacs. The robots, Berry had already experienced as the Night Comers. The computers, Tala told him, were thinking machines — machines that could think better than any man, which Berry found very hard to believe. The autofacs were a different kind of machine altogether. They could make things. They could make anything from clothing to robots, from weapons to music machines. Also in Faczone there were the hydros, where the fruit and vegetables were grown, the sea-tanks from which many kinds of sea-food were harvested, and the biofac which yielded many kinds of meat.

Parkzone was many times larger than Citizone and Faczone together. Indeed, said Tala, it was so big that unless you carried something called a transceiver, you could become lost in it and might die from heat or cold or lack of food and water or the attacks of wild animals. Berry was immediately interested in the possibilities of Parkzone. If a man could lose himself in such a place, it followed that, even if people or robots were sent to look for him, with cunning he might yet remain free. He questioned Tala closely. She had never

73

been in Parkzone and could only tell him what the Lady Sontag had told her.

Parkzone contained forests where strange animals roamed — creatures of which Berry had never heard. Lions, tigers, elephants, wolves, zebras, kangaroos, eland, wapiti, antelope and many others. In some of its rivers there were strange fish that could eat a man to the bone before his heart had ceased to beat. There were also animals called crocodiles that could bite a man in two by a single snap of the jaw.

But also in Parkzone there were snow-covered hills where the ristos liked to ski. Skiing was something that Berry could understand. The ristos fastened long smooth pieces of wood under their feet and slid down the snow slopes, taking much pleasure. Berry recalled that, as a child, he, too, had taken great pleasure in sliding along stretches of ice and snow during the cold season.

From what Tala said, it seemed to him that if he could somehow escape to Parkzone he might hide himself until he could make weapons and at least wreak some damage upon these peple who treated Earthside folk like animals. But there were so many difficulties, so many things he did not know.

His head ached continually.

Late on the third day, a robot came for both of them.

"Master, mistress, I am required to take you to the Controller. Will you come voluntarily?"

"We will come voluntarily," said Tala. She turned to Berry. "I fear our time together is ended. I fear also that for me — perhaps for both of us — much else is drawing to its close ... Did I please you, Berry, chief of the Londos?"

"You pleased me, Tala." Berry held her hand. "Be of good heart. The game is not played out."

Tala sighed. "I will try to believe that, my chief, though it is hard."

Berry was proud that she had used the words 'my chief'. It meant that she had freely given herself to the Londos clan.

Thirteen

THEY WERE TAKEN TO a place that was smaller than the hall in which Berry had first encountered Regis Le Gwyn. There were no women present, but besides the Controller there were three other men and two robots.

Regis Le Gwyn smiled. "So, Nothing-but-Berry, you have recovered from your first lesson, I see. I trust the second lesson was less painful and that the dirt female instructed you well."

This time, Berry was determined not to lose his temper. There was nothing to be gained by it — except perhaps another hole in the leg from the small sting weapon that Regis Le Gwyn doubtless still carried.

"I have learned much about this place from Tala," he said carefully. "She has told me all that she knows."

"And did she please you? Did you rut happily?"

Still Berry was not to be drawn. "She is much of a woman. I am content."

The Controller laughed. "It seems she has also taught you to be cautious, savage. Thus, having fulfilled her task, she may now be put down."

Berry looked at Tala. Her face had become white, and she trembled. He turned to the Controller. "Chief, what do you mean by these words 'put down'?"

Regis Le Gwyn exchanged glances with his companions. Once more he laughed. "Why, savage, they mean that she will be returned to Earth, that is all. You are concerned about the fate of this woman?"

"Yes, chief," said Berry patiently. "She is of my people, and I wish to know her destiny."

"Why, then, you know it, man." The Controller did not trouble to conceal his amusement. "Be content."

Berry knew that something was wrong, that somehow he was being tricked. Perhaps Tala was right. Perhaps the Earthside women were killed when they had served their purpose.

"Chief, I acknowledge your power, though I, too, am a chief in my own country. Will you give me your word that no harm will come to the woman Tala?"

"It is not necessary for me to give you my word about anything, savage," retorted Regis Le Gwyn, "as you must surely be aware. However, I am in an indulgent mood. I give you my word that the dirt woman will be returned to dirt."

Berry saw that the three men who were present found their chief's words amusing. He did not. The meaning was plain. Tala was right. They meant to kill her.

"Your word is not good enough, Regis Le Gwyn," he said. "You call me a savage. Perhaps I am. But I am not an animal. I have a mind which thinks. I know you may easily kill me; but until you do, you cannot stop the thoughts in my head. And if you do kill me now, all present will know that you, the Controller of Heaven Seven, were not clever enough to trick an ignorant savage . . . They may smile upon you, chief, as my clansmen smile upon me. But later they will think about what has passed. Later, they will say to themselves: The chief of our clan cannot trick a dirt savage. And when your back is turned, some ambitious man will point a weapon at it. So kill me now, chief. Now that I perceive your trickery. And your own time will surely come."

Regis Le Gwyn was white with fury. He gazed at his

companions. They did not return his gaze. They were staring at Berry in amazement.

Tala broke the tension. She threw herself at the Controller's feet. "My lord, do with me as you will. I know I have served my purpose and can be of no further use to you. But do not take vengeance upon this man Berry, I beg you. He knows not what he says. He is a clan chief, and he finds it hard to believe that the Controller of Heaven Seven is all-powerful. Be merciful. Surely, lord, there is some way he may yet serve you and live?"

Regis Le Gwyn looked down at her. He was grateful to Tala because she had diverted some embarrassment. The dirt savage — clearly a man of perception — had spoken the truth as he saw it. But the weapons already pointed at Regis Le Gwyn's back were not physical weapons. They were political weapons. There were many who would like to see a new Controller, and several who themselves aspired to that office. They would be skilful enough to use any apparent weakness to their own advantage.

Regis Le Gwyn looked down at Tala, displaying no sign of his gratitude. That, too, would have been interpreted as weakness. "So, dirt woman, you plead for him. That is interesting. You spend three years among a civilised people and learn something of their ways. Yet you plead for the life of a savage even when you are about to be put down. That is very interesting."

"Tala," said Berry gently, "have done. Get to your feet, woman, and be proud that you are Earth-born. This man, this Controller of Heaven Seven, is not a god. He is as powerful as his weapons and his people make him. Were I to encounter him alone, unarmed, he would step aside to let me pass."

Once more the Controller realised that Berry had simultaneously contrived to take the initiative and to insult him. "Savage, you are asking me to kill you!"

"No, chief," retorted Berry tranquilly, "I am daring you to kill me. These, your friends and servants, will remember your weakness."

Regis Le Gwyn was shaking visibly with anger. Berry noted his condition with some satisfaction. He noted also the looks on the faces of the Controller's companions. If I am to perish, he thought, Regis Le Gwyn will not remain chief of his clan for long. Those present have seen his weakness. They will tell his people.

"You will die," said the Controller. "Make no mistake, animal, you will die. But not here and now. Not quickly. Because that is what you want . . . You will die in an interesting fashion, slowly and in much agony. You will die in the forests of Parkzone. You will be eaten alive by the creatures of the forest. If any should attempt to give you a quick death it will be inhibited. A homing bee will follow wherever you go. It will observe and relay your sufferings, which I and others shall enjoy."

"Chief," retorted Berry, "I see that you are much afraid. You are a poor thing, not fit to be called a man. Remember that there are witnesses to what has passed between us and that my death will not ease your fear."

Before the Controller could speak, a robot said: "Lord, the Programmer approaches, requesting an immediate audience."

"The Programmer?" Regis Le Gwyn was discomfited. One moment he had been dwelling lovingly on the manner in which Berry would die. The next moment, he was informed that the Programmer — who rarely left Faczone, required an audience. He was so astounded that he failed to connect the two events. His inability to do so changed the course of history.

"Yes, Lord, the Programmer," confirmed the robot.

It would be possible to refuse the audience, of course,

or, at least, to defer it. But that would be the act of a braver man than Regis Le Gwyn. Nominally, the Controller had absolute power in Heaven Seven. But Regis Le Gwyn knew where the real power lay. It lay not in the hands of the Controller but in the hands of the man who led the teknos, who programmed the computers and therefore the robots, and who was responsible for the entire life-support systems of Heaven Seven.

Bors Zangwin, the Programmer, was a man whom Regis Le Gwyn had met in the flesh only on two previous occasions — at the chess tournaments which were the culmination of the Games. On each occasion, the Controller had been defeated in all ten matches though, among the ristos, he was the acknowledged Grand Master. Some of the ristos claimed that the Programmer had been taking computer advice. But, though a search was made, the judges found no bugs, relays or intercom devices at the table, in the salon or on the person of the Programmer himself, who had readily agreed to the search and, indeed, welcomed it.

As he contemplated the prospect of meeting the Programmer for the third time, Regis Le Gwyn was profoundly thankful that the next Games was seven years hence. If he suffered a third defeat, the political implications would be enormous.

"Let the Programmer be admitted," he said as calmly as possible. But it seemed to him that, even before he spoke, the door was opening and the Programmer was entering the chamber.

Bors Zangwin made the customary genuflexion. Yet his movements seemed insolent, almost imperious.

"Live long, Regis Le Gwyn," he said. "It is gracious of you to receive me."

The Controller licked his lips. "Live long, Bors Zangwin. It gives me pleasure to welcome you. To what do we owe this unexpected visit? Though I am most glad," he added hastily, "that you have ventured out of Faczone, if only for a short time."

Berry gazed at the newcomer. This Programmer wore garments vastly different from those of Regis Le Gwyn and the other ristos. Instead of their bright kilts, tunics and leg garments, he wore a dark robe that stretched from shoulders to ankle. And whereas the ristos affected long curled hair, the Programmer's head was close-cropped. Also, whereas Regis Le Gwyn had already shown that he was a man quick to anger, it seemed to Berry that the Programmer had the aspect of a man whose mind held sway over his emotions. If so, he could be a very dangerous man, perhaps more dangerous even than the Controller.

The inspection was mutual. While the Programmer spoke, his gaze flickered restlessly about. Most often, it came to rest upon Berry.

"I have an apology to offer and a favour to ask," said the Programmer, smiling at Regis Le Gwyn. "I hope you will accept the one and grant the other."

Regis Le Gwyn felt happier. The Programmer's voice was courteous, almost servile. That must surely mean that he now found himself in a delicate or difficult position.

"My dear Zangwin," said the Controller, "I cannot begin to imagine the circumstances under which you would find it necessary to apologise to me in person. As for the favour, if it is in my power to grant it without offending the laws to which we subscribe, be assured that is is already granted. Do you wish our conversation to continue in private?" He glanced at his companions as if to say: 'Look, this man is vulnerable and needs my help.'

But Bors Zangwin did not at all look vulnerable. He —

glanced at the Controller's companions coolly as if they were not ristos but nilskils. He looked at each of them, and none could meet his gaze.

"All present may remain," he said regally. "First, the apology, Controller. There has been a small fault — now fortunately traced — in the servomek system. It caused the robots' relay circuits to remain open. I am very sorry. The tekno responsible has been reprimanded by me and has lost ten years' seniority."

Regis Le Gwyn was nonplussed. Being an arts-oriented man, he knew nothing of relay circuits, open or closed. "What has this to do with me, my dear Programmer?" he enquired cautiously.

Bors Zangwin, who well knew that the Controller was unfamiliar with electronics, rewarded him with a condescending smile. "It is the reason for my sincere apology, Controller. Inadvertently, all situations where robots were present have been monitored, thus violating Article Fourteen of the Constitution which, as you know, is concerned with the right to privacy. Therefore, specifically, your encounter with these dirtside savages is at the moment on record. It will be erased, of course. I repeat: I am very sorry."

Regis Le Gwyn was sweating. Berry saw that he was sweating. So did the Programmer, so did the three ristos. Each derived satisfaction from the knowledge.

"This is inexcusable!" stormed Regis Le Gwyn, recalling that the playback — skilfully edited perhaps — would hardly show him in a favourable light.

"Inexcusable indeed," agreed the Programmer. "However, the tekno responsible has been severely punished, and I have apologised to you in person and before witnesses, as was proper. The record will be erased."

But Bors Zangwin did not seem at all apologetic. He had the air of one who was enjoying himself.

The Controller did his best to retrieve the situation. "I accept your apology," he said coldly. "The conversation was not of a significant or personal nature. The utterings of a demented dirtside creature are of little consequence to anyone ... You spoke of a favour, Programmer."

"I did — which you in your generosity have already granted, and for which I thank you."

Regis Le Gwyn looked briefly as if he might choke. But he managed to control himself. "It is my privilege to dispense favours to persons of lesser rank," he said insultingly, "always provided, as I said, that our laws are not offended. What is it you desire, Programmer?"

Bors Zangwin looked at Berry and Tala. "I request the custody of these dirtside people."

"They are not people, Programmer. They are savages, animals."

"Just so, Controller, if it is your pleasure to describe them as such."

Regis Le Gwyn felt himself to be on firm ground now. He had a queen's move to play which would give him the game and restore his authority in the sight of his risto companions.

"It is indeed my pleasure. May I enquire what interest the Programmer can have in such creatures?"

"It is my intention to investigate and analyse them in depth. It would be most useful to have complete psycho-files, including, of course, their male/female relationship. This will be of help in the project we have started to determine the long-term potential of Earthside people."

Regis Le Gwyn smiled. "Your project is commendable, Programmer. I greatly regret that it is impossible to release these savages for your investigations."

The Programmer raised an eyebrow. "Correct me if I have misinterpreted you, but I was under the impression that you had already and most graciously granted my request."

Regis Le Gwyn made his queen move. "I believe, my dear Programmer, that I did stipulate that it should not offend the laws to which we subscribe. The female is a three-term and therefore must be put down. The male, being judged dangerous, is under sentence of death, as you must know. Authority, as I am sure you will agree, must be maintained." Regis Le Gwyn enjoyed his queen's move. It was elegantly simple.

The Programmer shrugged. "You are right, as always, Controller. Authority must be maintained and the Constitution upheld. If the male is dangerous — and I do not doubt your judgment — then he must die, I suppose, in the manner you have prescribed, as an example. The female, having served her purpose, must also be put down. But is there any reason why execution should not be stayed until we teknos have had time to analyse these people?"

Berry, whose hopes had risen somewhat when the Programmer made his request, did not like the way things were now going. Better to be analysed, he thought — though he did not understand the term — and live a little longer than remain in the power of Regis Le Gwyn.

"I am glad you agree, Programmer, that Authority must be maintained and the Constitution upheld," said Regis Le Gwyn, unable to suppress a note of triumph in his voice. "Though I have great respect for your scientific interest in these dirtside creatures, I regret that there is no provision under our laws for the request you have made."

"With respect, there is," said Bors Zangwin, casually removing the Controller's queen. "Article Five."

"Article Five?" Regis Le Gwyn looked at him blankly.

"You are familiar with Article Five, of course," went

on the Programmer smoothly. "So I hope you will excuse me if I remind you unnecessarily of its wording. It states that the teknos have priority claim on any exobiological material for the purposes of analysis and evaluation. Demonstrably, these Earth people are exobiological material. In the interests of justice, Controller, our researches will be conducted with speed. I am sure you will be relieved to know that they do not offend the laws to which we dutifully subscribe."

Queen taken, attack destroyed, checkmate inevitable. Regis Le Gwyn could find nothing to say.

Bors Zangwin looked at Berry and Tala. "Will you come with me peacefully, or must I instruct robots to remove you?"

Berry glanced at Tala. Then he turned to the Programmer. "We will come peacefully, chief. I know not what you want with us, but likely it is preferable to death." He glanced at Regis Le Gwyn, now white with fury. Then Berry added slyly: "Also, chief, you appear to have great means of persuasion."

Fourteen

THE JOURNEY TO FACZONE was so full of marvels that
Berry's mouth fell open, his eyes bulged and he was at a
loss for words. He and Tala, accompanied only by Bors
Zangwin and one robot, were carried swiftly along in a
vessel whose shape was not unlike one of the large sea-
shells sometimes cast up by the tides of Earth. But it
did not appear to touch the ground over which it passed.
Also Berry observed many other shells, some following
them passing the one in which he sat, others apparently
rushing headlong towards it so that there must be a
dreadful collision. But there was none. The shells passed
each other closely; and after he had survived two such
encounters, Berry became convinced that death was not
imminent.

He was able to devote more attention to the strange
and sometimes awesome structures that were passed. Tala
remained silent, though she did not seem to be afraid
of the speed at which they were travelling, nor did she
seem greatly interested in the curious objects that flashed
by on either side of the vessel. No doubt she has seen
all this before many times, thought Berry. Also, she may
be afraid to speak in the presence of this chief who has
taken us, if for a short time, from certain death.

In fact, it was Bors Zangwin who provided Berry with
explanations. "We are travelling along Central Avenue
in Citizone," he told Berry. "These buildings that you
see are apartment blocks, restaurants, bars, theatres,

shops. All these terms will be explained to you later. For the time being, observe and remember." He pointed to a very tall building that seemed to dominate a square where trees grew, where there was a pool of water on which ducks and swans floated and where jets of water shot into the air to fall back like fine rain. "That is Citizone Hospital, where the sick and the injured are made whole. The smaller building by its side is the Psychiatric Centre, where people whose minds are sick go to be healed."

"Chief," said Berry, "you have taken us from a chief who seemed to be more powerful than you, but clearly is not. Why did you do this thing? I, too, am a chief in my own country. I have a right to know."

The Programmer smiled. "According to Regis Le Gwyn, Controller of Heaven Seven, you have no rights at all. You are a dirtside savage, an animal, and can be dealt with as such. I think otherwise. I will explain these matters to you presently. Meanwhile, will you trust me?"

Berry shrugged. "Chief, I have little choice. I know the power of your robots." He glanced at the streams of fast traffic on Central Avenue. "Also, it seems to me that a man who does not understand the ways of your country and the marvels therein may rapidly perish because of his ignorance."

Bors Zangwin laughed. "Berry, you are a practical and intelligent man. This pleases me and suits my intentions. We shall get on well together."

"You will not harm the woman Tala?"

"I will not harm Tala."

"Can you prevent her being put down, as Regis Le Gwyn calls it?"

"With your help, I believe I can."

"Then we shall help each other, Bors Zangwin.

Between me and Regis Le Gwyn there must be a reckoning."

Again, Bors Zangwin laughed. "I believe there will be, Berry. That is the purpose of my experiment."

The shell had left the streets and avenues of Citizone. Now it was passing into Faczone, a stark and austere place of great buildings with few windows, and with little traffic upon its avenues. But robots there were aplenty. As the shell speeded through Faczone, Berry saw more robots than people. It made him uneasy.

"Chief, is your clan composed more of robots than of people?"

The Programmer shook his head. "There is much for you to understand, Berry. Let us begin to penetrate the clouds of ignorance. It is true that there are far more robots than there are teknos. But the robots are not people, they are machines controlled by people . . . Have you used a bow and arrows?"

"Who has not?" asked Berry in surprise. "The bow is a favoured weapon among the clans."

"Then you will know that, unless a man fits an arrow to his bow and draws the string, releasing it when he has found a target, the arrow is useless."

Berry was amazed at this statement of the obvious. "But that is understood."

"Then understand, also," continued Bors Zangwin, "that the robots are as arrows, a computer is as the bow, and I am the man who holds the bow . . . Also, Berry, take your understanding a little further. Know that, if you are clever enough, it is my intention that you will be fashioned into a most deadly arrow and that I will draw the bow at a most dangerous target. Does the thought offend you?"

"Point me at the target," said Berry, "and, if the target is what I think, this arrow will fly true . . . But chief, when the arrow hits the target, what then? Will the bowman forget the shaft that served him well?"

"If there is a clean kill," said Bors Zangwin, "you will return to Earth, Berry, the woman Tala with you, the woman Vron also. But if the animal is only wounded, I cannot answer for the consequences."

"Just so," said Berry calmly. "A wounded animal in its frenzy is like to break the arrow that failed to find its heart . . . How did you know about Vron?"

"It is my business to know such things. But, see, we have reached Psycholab and there is work to be done. Time is not on our side, Berry. During the next nine days you will have little rest. The Controller, if I am not mistaken, will at this moment be discovering how long I can hold exobiological material before it must be returned to his jurisdiction. He will find that, by our laws, I can only retain it for ten days. So, we have nine days to educate you. On the tenth you must escape."

Psycholab was the place where Berry, a dirtside clansman, was destined to rediscover, in nine days, many of the skills and knowledge that had been lost upon Earth two thousand years ago.

Fifteen

HIS INTELLIGENCE QUOTIENT WAS 145; his performance quotient was 129; his talent quotient was 173. The result of the tests — all conducted on his first day in Faczone — showed that he was at near-genius level. The computer, already fed with the known details of Berry's background, had analysed the results against a mathematical model of his environmental history. The computer could not lie. Berry was outstanding. Bors Zangwin was more than satisfied.

"Tonight," he said, "you may spend with Tala, but the next seven nights you will spend alone. You will be sleeping, but you will not be resting. You will be learning much. The process will be explained to you. Now we will go to the refectory, where you will eat, and where you will meet some of the teknos who will help with your training."

The refectory was a large chamber not far from Psycholab. It had many windows, and it contained long tables at which teknos — all wearing long robes similar to that worn by the Programmer — sat eating their evening meal. All teknos had their hair close cropped; but some of them wore robes of a light colour. Looking at those in the lighter robes, Berry was amazed to discover from their shape and size that they were women.

When the Programmer entered the refectory, everyone present rose to their feet.

"Be seated, my friends," said Bors Zangwin. "Do not

let good food spoil... Was my interview with the Controller adequately monitored and recorded?"

"It was, Programmer," said someone.

"Good," said Bors Zangwin, rubbing his hands with satisfaction. "All who are concerned directly with Project Catalyst will present themselves in my reception chamber one hour from now."

A serving robot approached. "Master, will these people dine with you at high table?"

"They will. They will dine at high table so long as they remain with us."

The food was very good, Berry noted. Better than the food which had been given him and Tala during their brief imprisonment. Tala was seated on one side of the Programmer and Berry on the other. Each of them also sat next to another tekno and faced, across the table, three more.

Bors Zangwin talked more than he ate. First he made introductions.

"This, comrades, is the Earth man, Berry, who will be the subject of our experiment and who will, I hope, be the trigger mechanism that changes the balance of power and brings our aims to fulfilment. And this is the dirtside female— I beg your pardon, Tala — the Earth woman who has initiated his orientation... Berry, the man sitting next to you is Oros van Skut, grade two tekno, psychologist of distinction. The woman sitting next to Tala is Mabula Daxinska, also grade two, our electro-analyst. The men facing you are Laris Bonteil, grade three psychoprogrammer; Jorj Minchos, grade three hypnologist; and Sun Yat Sen, grade three medic. These five are the people who will transform you in a few days from a man of one world into a man of two worlds. If all goes well, Berry, you will be a formidable person. You will be unique. You will be the first man of our time to combine the lore of Earth with the skills and knowledge we have developed in Heaven Seven."

"Chief," said Berry, "I understand little of what you say. I know only that you have saved me — if for a short time — from the vengeance of Regis Le Gwyn, who is a weak man though he holds much power. I know not what you wish to achieve — except," he added with a smile, "that it concerns greater matters than the discomfort or destruction of one who is known to be of poor spirit."

"Aha! You see!" Bors Zangwin gazed triumphantly at his teknos. "This man, whom the Controller dismisses as a dirtside savage, an animal, is astute, is he not?"

"Also, chief," went on Berry calmly, "it occurs to me that if my success in this as yet unknown venture could bring about the defeat of the Controller and, perhaps, the risto clan, my failure may achieve a similar result for yourself and these good teknos."

Bors Zangwin laughed aloud. "You see! You see! He reasons well."

"Therefore, chief," continued Berry, "it seems to me that I, too, hold some power, though I am far from my clan and," he glanced at Tala, "almost alone."

The Programmer gazed at him intently. "That is true. Project Catalyst cannot exist without your co-operation, Berry. Or, to be more exact, if you refuse to co-operate, the project will have to wait until we can acquire another Earthside male with similar potential."

Berry smiled. "In which case, chief, we may strike a bargain, since each of us needs the help of the other."

"What kind of bargain do you have in mind?"

"A simple one. Through me — though I do not yet know how — you wish to strike at an enemy who is my enemy also. This project, as you call it, holds much danger for me but less, I think, for you. Therefore I ask you in the presence of these, your people, to give me your word that, should I die, you will find a way to return Tala, Vron and the rest of the women from my clan to Earth."

Bors Zangwin stroked his chin. "You ask much."

"I know, chief. But I think you ask much of me also. So far as I can, I will do what you require. Will you, before these your people, say the same?"

"How do you know that I would keep my word?"

"I do not. But I know that the chief of a clan must be honest before his people, else they will not be honest before him."

"Berry, you have much wisdom. Here in Heaven Seven we have many skills, but, perhaps, not a great deal of wisdom. We have need of people like you — which was why Project Catalyst was conceived ... You have my word, then. In the event of your death, we will do all that is possible to return Tala, Vron and the Londos women to earth. If you should fail, this effort will cost us dearly. But we will try."

Berry held out his hand. "I believe you, chief, and am content. It is a good bargain."

The Programmer clasped his hand. "Make it a better one. Do not fail ... Now let us waste no more time. Finish your meal quickly, Berry, then we and the teknos concerned with this project will meet at the briefing. There you will learn what is expected of you. Let us hope it is not too much."

Berry gazed tranquilly at his plate. "You serve good meat, Bors Zangwin. A man cannot but gain strength on food such as this."

Sixteen

THE BRIEFING WAS LARGELY for the benefit of Berry. Apart from himself and Tala, there were nine teknos present. The meeting took place in a circular room that had no windows in its walls but a great circular, transparent window in its ceiling. The light outside was fading. Berry gazed up with wonder and pleasure as the stars began to appear. He tried to imagine that he was at a fire-talk on Earth.

The Programmer noticed his gaze. "Beautiful, are they not? A most satisfying illusion, Berry. Those are not real stars, but images projected upon the dome that protects Heaven Seven from the deadly vacuum of space."

Berry said nothing. He did not understand what a dome was or what the vacuum of space was; and the stars looked convincingly real. But he could think of no reason why Bors Zangwin should lie to him about such things. And he marvelled anew at the skills of these people who lived on an island in the sky.

The Programmer said: "With the exception of our Earthside companions, all here are familiar with the aims of Project Catalyst. But, so that Berry shall understand the situation and realise what we expect of him, I will give a brief resumé.

"As you know, Heaven Seven was stabilised in its present form one thousand seven hundred and ninety-three years ago when the last of the orbiting stations was incorporated into our closed system. After that time, a social structure evolved which became static more than a thousand years ago.

"Originally, the social structure was based upon the development of an élite. But, because of nepotism and other factors, a caste society is the end product. A caste society consisting of ristos, teknos and nilskils. Why cannot this society change into something more fluid, more creative? Because long ago, the ristos had it written into the Constitution that they were the only people entitled to procreate. They, being the most creative and talented people, were to provide the genetic pool. Those of their children who showed little promise would, theoretically, remain nilskils until they died. Those who showed greater promise, particularly in the sciences, would become teknos — who could not be a threat to the oligarchy because they were a selected group denied the privilege of procreation.

"The system might have continued to work but for two main factors: nepotism and cosmic radiation. That is to say, of course, that it might have continued to work to the advantage of the ristos. For, despite the scientific methods we teknos developed for the evaluation of intelligence, talent and performance, the ristos continued to absorb into their caste only those people whom they themselves evaluated by non-scientific method and subjective criteria.

"The nepotism we might have continued to tolerate, because none of us — nilskils and teknos alike — can forget that we are the offspring of risto union. This genetic loyalty was and is the real strength of the ristos.

"But the long-term effects of cosmic radiation must override genetic loyalty. It became apparent many generations ago that the incident of pre-natal and post-natal abnormalities was increasing steadily and would continue to increase until the civilisation we have tried to preserve is destroyed. Many of my predecessors warned many of the previous controllers, as I have warned Regis Le Gwyn. But to no effect.

"The only reasonable solution to the problem is that we of Heaven Seven must return to Earth before it is too late. But the ristos know that if this happens life will be very hard for them — as it is for Berry and his people — and, more important, that they will inevitably lose their supremacy. Their solution — if that is what it can be called — consists simply of accepting the rise in foetal abnormalities and importing more and more Earth women to carry the fertilised risto ova.

"They forget or choose to ignore the law of diminishing returns. The more Earth women they take, the more they reduce future supplies of Earth women. Further, the supply of Heavenside ova is finite, as we all know. But, regardless of our partial success in the field of cosmic ray deflection, the increase in foetal abnormalities remains unchecked. At present we recycle five out of every six live births. Soon it will be six out of every seven. Within my lifetime — unless I die by violent means — it will be nine out of ten.

"What is the answer? Revolution? We teknos have great power at our disposal. But we are few in number. Also, the ristos are not without skilled and intelligent people. And let us not forget that they can still command the loyalty of more than ninety per cent of the nilskils.

"The only possible solution is to discredit the ristos. They consider themselves to be the élite of human evolution. They regard Berry and his people as animals and treat Earth women as brood mares. But what if one of these dirtside animals were to prove that he was as intelligent and resourceful as the best of the ristos? What if Berry outwitted Regis Le Gwyn and discredited him? The myth of risto superiority would be destroyed for ever

Even the nilskils would no longer offer blind allegiance. There would be a bloodless revolution that would pave the way for a recolonisation of Earth.

"That, my friends, is the essence of Project Catalyst. You know your assigned tasks. Perform them with optimum speed and efficiency."

The Programmer paused and looked at Berry. "I am sorry that I have had to use words and ideas that may be difficult for you to understand now. But soon you will remember what I have said and be able to understand it perfectly."

"My head aches somewhat," admitted Berry. "But I have learned much that is useful. I have learned that you of Heaven Seven, like we of Earth, are a divided people. I have learned that you cannot remain for ever on this island in the sky; because if you do, you are doomed. This is important to me, since it means there is yet hope for the clans. So, give me the skills that I need, and I will make Régis Le Gwyn very sorry that he and his kind have ill-used the women of Earth and have treated a clan chief like an animal." He yawned. "And now I am tired. If this is to be my last night of peace for a time, I would make the best use of it. Give me leave to rest, Programmer. Tomorrow I shall work hard at the task of becoming a fatal arrow."

"You will wish to share the night with Tala?"

Berry grinned. "It is strange, but I have my best thoughts when I lie with a woman."

Seventeen

AFTER THEIR NIGHT TOGETHER — which, Berry supposed, might well be the last he spent in the arms of an Earth woman — he saw Tala only at meal times in the refectory. Bors Zangwin did not approve of this because he felt it might disturb Berry's concentration. But Berry demanded to see Tala regularly as a guarantee of good faith, so that he could be sure she was not being ill-treated in any way. He asked if he could see Vron also, but the Programmer explained that this was beyond his power.

Vron had been assigned to a risto called the Lady Somavalt and would remain a child-bearing proxy until she had carried the statutory three. The Programmer did not tell Berry that an Earth child — Berry's child — had been removed from her womb so that it could be prepared for the reception of one of the Lady Somavalt's fertilised ova. Nor did he mention that Vron was in shock and under sedation. These matters would definitely have disturbed Berry's concentration.

On the first morning, under hypnosis, Berry absorbed a programmed crash course in modern terrestrial history. It began with the brush wars of the late twentieth century, passed on to the population crisis of the early twenty-first century, then to the period during which the reserves of fossil fuels became exhausted, to the crumbling of technologically advanced cultures and to the inevitable nuclear conflict. He learned how and why the great civilisations had perished, leaving behind a comparatively few hardy survivors who eventually established the culture of the clans.

Tala was surprised when, at lunch, Berry, none the worse for his hypno-learning, tried to explain to her why the hot spots existed on Earth and how the once great power blocs, having become politically unstable because of their starving populations, were driven to mutual destruction. Bors Zangwin listened to the account with some satisfaction. Berry had been programmed only with facts. But here he was evaluating those facts, interpreting their significance, judging personalities long dead, forming opinions on events long past. Truly, his Q ratings had been conservatively estimated by the psycomputer.

In the afternoon he was again medically and psychologically tested. The results showed that his health remained good, that his performance quotient and talent quotient remained stable but that his intelligence quotient strangely had increased seven points. During the late afternoon he was given first the basic maths programme then the advanced.

At the evening meal he confused Tala greatly when he tried to explain the significance of Operator J — the square root of minus one.

During the night, sleepteach gave him general games theory, the principles of chess, and the habits, customs and laws of the culture that had developed in Heaven Seven.

At breakfast — taken as all meals were, at the high table — Berry remarked to Bors Zangwin that chess was a fascinating game, not unlike the game of chief stone, played by some of the old men of the clans.

"Would you like to play me at chess, Berry?"

Berry smiled. "It would be an interesting contest, chief."

"Then I will send for pieces and a board. We may play as we eat."

Berry looked faintly surprised. "There is no need. Can we not play with our minds only?"

It was the turn of Bors Zangwin to look surprised. "Very well. You are white."

"King's pawn to K4," said Berry without hesitation.

"A naïve opening," said the Programmer.

Berry shrugged. "I am a simple man."

"King's pawn to K4 also," said the Programmer. "I shall be interested to observe your intentions."

Berry feinted for a fool's mate he knew that Bors Zangwin would not let him have. The Programmer countered with a queen defence, then followed with a knight attack that forced Berry to move his own queen and cost him an unprotected pawn, at the same time giving Bors Zangwin an opportunity to bracket king and castle.

Berry looked at the Programmer in some embarrassment. "I am sorry, chief. I hoped to do better."

Bors Zangwin regarded him benignly. "You will do better. This is only your first game."

After that Berry began to lose pieces rapidly under remorseless attack. But it took the Programmer seventeen moves to get a checkmate. He was surprised at the way Berry contrived to avoid disaster for so long.

Tala looked at the two men in astonishment. She knew nothing of chess and could not understand how a game could be played by the opponents simply declaring their moves to each other.

"Chief, I am sorry," said Berry. "I will give you a better game next time."

"Today you will work hard and learn much," said the Programmer. "Tomorrow, at breakfast, we will play again. There will be a board and pieces."

"It will not be so easy for you."

"I am sure it won't ... Berry, your progress is being continuously evaluated and analysed. It is better than I had hoped."

"Thank you, chief."

"Thank you, Berry."

That morning, Berry was medically and psychologically tested once more. The three quotients remained stable. Later in the morning he was programmed in basic physics.

At lunch, he tried to explain to Tala how it was possible for Heaven Seven to remain in permanent orbit round the Earth.

She was frightened. "Berry, what are they doing to you? You are no longer the clan chief I knew. Your mind is changing. I am afraid."

"Be not afraid," he said equably. "Despite the wonders of programmed learning, analysis, sleepteach, hypnoteach and computer testing, I am still the same man of the forest. *I* do not change, Tala. My knowledge and understanding increases. That is all." He turned to Bors Zangwin. "This is so, is it not?"

"It is so," agreed the Programmer. "But I think the new knowledge will affect your attitudes and beliefs, though your personality remains the same ... Apart from what I hope it will achieve, this experiment in crash learning is of great scientific interest. We shall discover much simply by studying your reactions."

Berry was surprised. "You have not tried it before?"

Bors Zangwin smiled. "It is illegal — at least, for Heavenside people. The ristos framed the Constitution, as you know, and they were clever enough to realise that we teknos might one day develop artificial methods for increasing intelligence. In which case, of course, it would be possible to culture an intellectual élite. Such an élite might then form a new power bloc — to the discomfort of the ristos." He sighed. "However, we teknos have sworn to uphold the Constitution and to abide by its laws. This we do. If it could be shown that we did not, the ristos could mobilise the nilskils — over seventy per cent of Heaven Seven's population— against us. The consequences of that are unforseeable. We, as you know, hold scientific power. But we do not have moral power, political power. The ristos and the nilskils are united in their distrust of the teknos. Therefore we rigorously observe the law ... Fortunately, it is not unlawful to experiment with exobiological material. Is this clear to you?"

"Excellently clear," said Berry, helping himself to more meat. "What is the best you hope for in this experiment on exobiological material?"

"That you will integrate the knowledge you have acquired and put it to good use — not only for your personal survival, but for the survival of your people and mine."

"What is the worst that you fear?"

Bors Zangwin regarded him calmly. "That you will go mad before the experiment is completed."

"I shall not go mad," said Berry. "Would you care for a game of chess?"

"There is not much time before your next session."

"Then we may play quickly."

"Shall I send for a board and pieces?"

"No, chief. Let us play with our minds, as before."

Berry was checkmated on the twenty-third move. It did not seem to worry him. "I am improving, chief."

"Demonstrably so. If you had not exposed your queen. . ."

"Chief, I will not make the same mistake again."

"I believe you."

Bors Zangwin was elated. Tala succeeded in holding back her tears.

Eighteen

DURING THE NINE FULL days that Berry remained in the care of the teknos, his 'education' was completed. He had absorbed maths and the basic sciences. Then he had been given ancillary sciences — electronics, bionics, cybernetics theory — as well as a grounding in psychology, anthropology and sociology. He had not left Faczone, but he had been programmed with a detailed knowledge of Citizone and the habits and customs of the ristos and nilskils. He had also been programmed with the lay-out of Parkzone and with knowledge of the great variety of wildlife to be encountered there.

During the entire crash course, Berry had been regularly subjected to medical examination, to psychological tests and to Q tests. Though his appetite remained good and he ate exceedingly well, he lost four kilos in weight. This was ascribed to the intense neural stimulation to which he was constantly subjected. By the fourth day, the skin under his eyes was dark with fatigue and he displayed signs of irritability and nervous tension. Mild tranquillisers were introduced into his diet. The darkness under his eyes remained, but the irritability and tension decreased somewhat.

At meal times, he continued to challenge the Programmer to games of chess. Chess, it seemed, fascinated him to the point where it was almost becoming an addiction.

When Bors Zangwin questioned him about this compulsive desire to play, he said: "It is a form of individual combat — subtle and exciting — wherein neither opponent is hurt. It is a combat to the death without anyone dying — except, of course, the king." Then he smiled slyly and added: "Also, chief, it is a means whereby a man may learn much of the way his enemy thinks."

"Do you regard me as your enemy?" enquired Bors Zangwin.

Berry contrived to look shocked. "Only in the matter of chess. You have shown me great kindness. You have opened my mind. In this game of chess only, I think, are you my enemy."

"I hope so," said Bors Zangwin. "But I am reminded of the ancient myth of a man called Franken Stein who created a monster. Shall we play?"

"Yes, chief, let us play."

On the fifth day, it took the Programmer twenty-seven moves to checkmate Berry.

On the sixth day it took him thirty-two moves.

On the seventh day, Berry fought to a stalemate.

On the eighth day, Berry won a close-run game in thirty-nine moves.

On the ninth day, the Programmer resigned after Berry's nineteenth move, which relieved him of his queen and made checkmate seem inevitable.

"Why did you resign, chief?" Berry successfully kept the note of triumph out of his voice.

Bors Zangwin shrugged. "Defeat was inevitable. I congratulate you."

Berry smiled. "I thought you might try for a stalemate."

The Programmer said: "It was hopeless — a chance in a thousand. You would have had to make two critical errors."

"I might have made them, chief."

"I doubt it."

"Even so, it might have happened. I have seen men destroyed by their own confidence ... That is the difference between us. I would have taken the chance in a thousand."

The Programmer laughed. "Perhaps that is where you have the advantage, Berry, you and your kind. We of Heaven Seven have always enjoyed security, whereas you Earthside people live with death or disaster as a constant threat. Perhaps we have much to learn from you ... I will say this now. I have enjoyed your society. You have done better than I had hoped."

"You think, then, you have fashioned a good arrow?"

Bors Zangwin looked at him keenly. "I do. The material from which it is constructed is excellent, and the craftsmen were not without skill. But perhaps the arrow will not fly precisely as the bowman intended."

"The only way to discover that, chief, is to draw the bow."

"Enough of metaphors. Regis Le Gwyn has communicated with me. He left it till late, hoping to surprise me. I thought he would. He requires that I surrender the exobiological material I requisitioned for experimental use at mid-day tomorrow."

"Will you obey him?"

The Programmer seemed surprised by the question. "I will obey the law, Berry. We teknos are vulnerable, as you know. We must always obey the law."

"That is as I thought. Do you wish to know my plans?"

"From now on, I wish to know nothing at all of your thoughts or intentions." The Programmer smiled. "I doubt also that you would tell me."

Berry also smiled. "I may have lied somewhat. Sometimes it is wise to mislead even a friend."

"I do not doubt it . . . Perhaps, as this is your last night in Faczone, you would wish to share it with Tala."

"That is kind of you, chief."

"The door to your chamber will be locked, as usual, of course. We have to be able to show that normal precautions were taken. Also, as usual, a robot will be on duty outside the door in case some emergency arises."

"Naturally," said Berry. "That is understood."

The Programmer examined his finger-nails. "The experiment has been a great success. Our records will show that an Earthside person is potentially as good as a Heavenside person. This is a significant and gratifying result . . . Incidentally, do you know where my private chamber is?"

"I do, chief."

Bors Zangwin, having finished examining his finger-nails, turned his gaze to the ceiling and spoke almost as if to himself. "I really must remember to lock the door. Of course, no tekno would enter it without permission. But there are occasions when strangers — apart from yourself — visit Faczone. Frequently, we have groups of nilskils who are hoping for tekno rating; and, now and then, there is the odd sight-seeing risto. Of course, it is hardly likely that such people would presume to enter the Programmer's private chamber uninvited. But I should be careful, I suppose."

"You should, indeed," agreed Berry gravely.

The Programmer appeared not to have heard him. "Though, of course, the only valuables there are my favourite hunting laser — with which I was once foolish enough to destroy a hippopotamus in Parkzone — my multichannel transceiver and, I think, some lightweight food concentrates which we have recently developed and which have yet to be fully proved . . . Perhaps I worry too much. I cannot imagine who would be tempted to take such things."

"Nor can I, chief."

The Programmer appeared to recall Berry's presence. "I have many administrative matters to attend to. Goodbye, Berry, until we meet again — if we do. I have learned much from you."

"Farewell, chief. I think we shall meet again. I have learned much also, and am grateful."

Nineteen

WHEN BERRY WAS ALONE with Tala, he told her of his final encounter with the Programmer.

"Then we are no better off," said Tala, "except that we have lived a little longer. Tomorrow, the robots will take us back to Citizone, and that will be an end of it."

"Not so, Tala. We leave this place tonight. Most of the teknos are now asleep. I believe that on this night they will be less inclined to pay attention to strange noises than formerly. Then we will challenge Regis Le Gwyn to seek us in a place of our choosing."

"How can that be? The door is locked, and outside a robot stands guard. Have these teknos taught you to pass through a locked door and defeat a creature of metal?"

"I already knew how to use my wits," retorted Berry. "The teknos have shown me how to use their skills. That is enough. See what I have taken from the chamber of Bors Zangwin." He withdrew the laser pistol, the compact transceiver and two packs of food concentrate from the inside pockets of his tunic.

Tala was horrified. "But these things will be missed, and the teknos will know that only you would steal them."

"I think not," said Berry confidently. "For a time, at least, Bors Zangwin will look the other way."

"What does that mean?"

"It means that he is in no hurry to see the Controller

of Heaven Seven destroy us. Now listen carefully. I will short-circuit the electromagnetic lock on the door. As soon as we are outside the chamber, I will hit the robot's communication circuit so that it cannot report what is happening. Then I will hit its visual system so that it cannot see. We must then go to the commissariat and take two tekno robes, one for you and one for me. After that, we will find the nearest air-car and I will programme it to take us to Parkzone."

Tala looked at him in wonder. "You can do these things?"

"These and much more . . . You wish to live, Tala? Remember that you are a dirtside third-term female. If we are caught your doom is certain."

"I wish to live," she said simply.

"Then obey me without question, that is all."

"I will, my chief."

Berry let out a great sigh. "I promise nothing, you understand. We may not live much longer. But if we do not, I think many ristos will die regretting that they thought of us as dirtside animals."

Tala sighed also. "That is something."

Berry put the transceiver and the food concentrate back into his pocket. Then he went to the door and examined the lock intently for a moment or two.

"When the door is open, we must move quickly and silently," he whispered. "Simply follow me when I have dealt with the robot."

He took the laser pistol and triggered a brief burst of radiance at the wall close to the lock. Plastic melted, burned and gave off acrid smoke. There was a muffled click as hidden wires melted and the electromagnet released the locking rod.

Berry opened the door rapidly and stepped out of the chamber.

"Master, you —" began the robot.

With the pistol set at full power, Berry lasered the robot's chest panel, behind which the communication circuitry lay. Then, without cutting the beam, he swept it upwards to the more exposed lens systems. Spectacularly, the robot's visor burst into flame. With an oddly human gesture, the robot put up its hands as if to ward off further attack, dropped them, spun round, walked briskly into the wall, and fell down.

Berry did not stay to observe further antics.

"Come!" He took Tala's hand and raced down the corridor, pulling at her relentlessly when she flagged.

They got out of the dormitory building without encountering any more robots or any teknos. Berry looked up at the 'sky' — clear with many stars, bright with an almost full moon — and briefly cursed at the ability of the teknos to present such a convincing illusion. He had hoped that they would have programmed a dull and cloudy night for his escape. But perhaps that would have been too obvious a sign of assistance.

Acutely conscious that he and Tala were clearly visible to any watchers, Berry sped to the commissariat, a high and slender building, cylindrical in shape, with no windows. The doors were not locked. Theft was a rare event in Heaven Seven, and especially so in Faczone.

He half-expected to find service robots on duty, but he saw none.

He punched the lift control for level three, where all garments made in the cyberfax were automatically delivered and stored. The tekno robes, thick, durable and hooded, were all stored in one area. He and Tala quickly found robes that fitted. For a moment or two, Berry also debated the possibility of taking some risto clothes as well. Then he decided against it. Risto clothing was too conspicuous. Also he had learned that most ristos preferred handmade garments — indeed, couture was a favoured risto art-form. Therefore any risto who wore cyberfax clothes might attract attention.

When he and Tala had transformed themselves into inconspicuous teknos, they went down to level two where tools, Games equipment, implements and instruments were stored. There he equipped Tala with a hatchet, a hunting knife and an anaesthetic gun. He took for himself three light Games javelins, a Games crossbow and bolts. The Programmer's laser pistol was a fine weapon; but Berry, though now educated in the skills of Heaven Seven, remained a man of Earth, a man of the forest. He trusted the weapons he had chosen because they were simple. If the laser pistol developed a fault, he would have no means of repairing it. If its power supply became exhausted it would just be useless metal and crystal.

"Let us go," he said. "This matter between myself and Regis Le Gwyn will not be settled as the ristos think. It will be settled in the manner of Earth." He laughed quietly. "The ristos like to hunt. We will see how well they liked to be hunted."

Tala shivered. "Berry, I sometimes think that all the teknos have done to you has made you mad."

He took her hand. "Be not afraid. They have only opened my mind."

Outside the commissariat all was quiet. There were still no robots to be seen.

But he found an air-car close to the building. He was sure it had not been there before they had entered. He smiled. Bors Zangwin, it seemed, did not sleep so deeply as he had supposed.

When he and Tala boarded the car, he noticed that the programme panel already had a destination punched on its keys: CA10-27. The 27th residence on 10th Avenue in Citizone. If he did not reprogramme for

Parkzone, if he simply pressed the go key, the car would take him to that address.

He thought for a moment or two, then turned to the reference panel. He dialled the Directory code — briefly wondering how he knew it, then realising it had probably been given him in sleepteach — and, having engaged the circuit, dialled the programmed destination. Directory revealed on the view screen that CA10-27 was the home of a female risto: the Lady Somavalt.

"There is a slight variation in my plan," said Berry. "Before we seek refuge in Parkzone, we go to visit a risto, the Lady Somavalt."

"Why, Berry? Why do you add to the dangers that beset us?"

"I wish to reclaim a woman of Earth, Tala, a woman of the Londos. My woman. Do you object?"

Tala let out a great sigh. "No, my chief. I, too, am now a woman of the Londos. Also I am your woman. It shall be as you wish."

Berry pressed the go key and set the car for fast drive. As it accelerated rapidly out of Faczone, he reflected that Bors Zangwin was a very remarkable man.

Twenty

THE LADY SOMAVALT EVIDENTLY had guests. Several
air-cars were parked in the avenue beside her house,
which was a replica — as Berry recognised — of a
twentieth century Swiss chalet. Even most of the ristos
lived in apartment blocks. The Lady Somavalt was,
apparently, a very influential person.

Light came from all the windows of the chalet, and
there was the sound of music and laughter. A house robot
was on duty by the door.

"Stay in the car," Berry told Tala. "I have programmed
it for Entrance Five of Parkzone. I am now entering this
house. If you find yourself in danger before I return,
press this key. When you reach Parkzone, hide yourself
and give a good accounting when they come to look for
you."

"I understand, my chief. This woman, Vron, she means
much to you?"

"Yes. You also mean much to me," said Berry
patiently. "Now, whatever happens, do not leave the car."

"I will obey. Already you have extended my life."

Berry got out of the car and walked to the chalet door.
The robot said: "Your invitation, master. The Lady
Somavalt requires all cards to be presented before entry.
I was not programmed to expect a tekno."

"I was not programmed to be a tekno," retorted Berry.
He took out the laser pistol, fused the robot's communication circuits, knocked out the visual system, then des-

troyed its co-ordination centre so that it could not thresh about. Then he went quickly to each of the parked cars and lasered its control panel. Judging from the number of cars, he estimated that there would be not less than six and probably not more than twenty guests in the house. He did not know how many residents there would be; but he did know that, apart from serving robots and proxy wombs — as the risto women called their Earthside slaves — ristos tended to live alone.

The Lady Somavalt was holding a dinner party. It was a rather special dinner party because among her guests was the Controller of Heaven Seven. Most of the other guests were close friends, male and female, of Regis Le Gwyn. This was Somavalt's way of saying thank you for having been allocated a tenth proxy womb when most risto ladies in her ageing sequence had been allowed no more than seven or eight. Regis Le Gwyn had never asked her to open for him. But this evening, she felt, he might. Particularly after the psychedelics, and if the vibes were right. The tekno who had been bribed to supply her with the new erotic skin dressing — not yet generally released because of some stupid regulation that concerned the proving of its non-toxic effect — had assured her that no man could resist it. Somavalt greatly wanted a child by Regis Le Gwyn. It would consolidate her position as one of the top twenty.

She was reflecting upon this pleasant prospect when suddenly a madman wearing the robe of a tekno burst into the dining chamber, instantly lasered the circuits of one of the two serving robots, then turned his pistol on Regis Le Gwyn.

There were screams, shouts, looks of terror and incredulity.

"Let no one move," said Berry, "or this man dies." He

nodded towards the Controller, whose face had gone deathly pale.

A woman was the first to recover her wits. "Who — who are you? Why have you done this? What do you want?"

Berry ignored her. He was gratified to see that the other robot remained still, not wishing to endanger the humans.

"I seek the Lady Somavalt. I do not intend to harm her."

"I am the Lady Somavalt." It was the same woman. He looked at her. She was very beautiful, very much a woman even by Earth standards, though somewhat thin.

"Lady, do you have an Earth woman in this house — a recent arrival?"

"Yes."

"Her name?"

"Vron."

"That is the one. Outside there is a car with a tekno in it. Instruct your robot to take the woman Vron out to the car. If this is done rapidly, all here will live. If not, Regis Le Gwyn will be the first to die."

The Lady Somavalt blanched. "She has been ill. She is weak and under sedation."

"Even so, let it be done. Let the robot wrap her and carry her. And let it be done quickly. I am indifferent to the fate of ristos."

"Who are you?"

Berry glanced at the Controller. "He can tell you. But if you do not give the order quickly, he will not live long enough."

The Lady Somavalt looked at the remaining robot. "Do with the proxy womb as he says — and hurry!"

"Yes, my Lady."

"Robot," said Berry, "your circuits are undamaged

and you have doubtless relayed the situation to computer control."

"Yes, master."

"Now obey the instructions of the Lady Somavalt with much speed. Return here when your task is accomplished."

Regis Le Gwyn seemed to recover some courage. "You will pay for this, savage — as will Bors Zangwin, who has clearly betrayed us."

"So, chief," said Berry, "you are brave enough to look at a laser pistol and make threats. That is something. Perhaps you are almost a man, after all. But do not trouble yourself greatly about the Programmer. He has already paid somewhat. I have taken much that he values."

"Who is this mad creature?" demanded Somavalt desperately. The evening which she had planned so carefully and on which she had spent so much thought was utterly destroyed. She knew now, with dreadful clarity, that no proxy womb of hers would ever bear a child sired by Regis Le Gwyn.

"He is a dirtside savage," said the Controller. "His name is Berry." He gave a faint smile. "Nothing-but-Berry. It seems that we of Heaven Seven have underestimated him."

"You have, indeed chief," said Berry. "I gave you my word that there would be a reckoning between us. The time draws close, but it will not be tonight." He turned to the guests. "I call all here to witness that I, Berry, chief of the Londos people of Earth, challenge Regis Le Gwyn to mortal combat with such weapons as he chooses. It will be interesting to see how the Controller of Heaven Seven fares against a dirtside savage, will it not?"

Regis Le Gwyn, mindful of the laser, tried to control

his fury. "I will not fight you, savage. I will hunt you as I would hunt an animal."

"Just so," said Berry. "Remember that all here have witnessed your promise. Do not break it. A chief who breaks his word loses the respect of his people."

The robot returned. "Master, the proxy womb has been placed in the air-car with the tekno."

"Thank you," said Berry, and lasered his vision circuit.

He turned to the Lady Somavalt. "Lady, I am sorry to interrupt your feast, but it may continue presently. I require your presence as a hostage so that I may have safe conduct to my destination. Please go out to the air-car. Do not make trouble. The tekno is armed. You have my word that if we are not intercepted you will be released very soon. Also," he smiled, "you will then be able to inform the Controller of my destination. I think he will be interested."

Somavalt looked at her guests appealingly. Most avoided her gaze. But one young man leaped to his feet and glared angrily not at Berry but at the Controller. "This is monstrous! Can you not stop it?"

Berry lasered the fleshy part of his shoulder. The young man fell back to his chair, groaning.

"Lord, I asked you not to move," said Berry. "Do you value the life of your chief so little?" He looked at the Lady Somavalt. "Lady, unless you obey me quickly, Regis Le Gwyn is a dead man. Since he has accepted my challenge, this would cause me some disappointment. Doubtless I would learn to bear it . . . I repeat: you have my word that you will not be harmed. But decide now, Lady, for I grow impatient."

Pale, her breasts heaving, the Lady Somavalt rose shakily to her feet and went out of the chamber.

"I require that you, Regis Le Gwyn, command these, your people, to do nothing until the Lady Somavalt returns to tell you where I have gone. If there is any pursuit, she will die. I am a man of my word, as you must now know. Speak!"

Regis Le Gwyn glanced at his fellow guests. He did not like the expressions he saw on their faces. Whatever else happened, he knew that there would soon be a new Controller.

He faced Berry. "Savage, there will be no pursuit until I am sure that the Lady Somavalt is safe. After that, you would be wise to kill yourself quickly."

Berry laughed. "Courage, indeed! Well spoken. Let the witnesses take note."

Then he lasered the lighting panels and, as the chamber was plunged into darkness, made his exit.

Twenty-one

WHEN BERRY HAD LEFT Faczone most of the teknos
had retired to bed. But, as the air-car sped through
Citizone, Berry noticed that there were still numbers of
nilskils and ristos about and a steady flow of air-cars
along the streets and avenues. Customarily, the teknos
rose early and worked long. But many nilskils and most
ristos disdained such regularity. Basically, Berry realised,
they were parasites supported by the hard-working teknos
and an automated economy. No wonder the comparatively small group of the teknos resented the situation.
No wonder that Bors Zangwin had developed Project
Catalyst.

I will be more than a catalyst, thought Berry. These
people of Heaven Seven are already divided among themselves. I will divide them yet further.

He was pleased that there was still some traffic in
Citizone. It would render the passage of his air-car less
conspicuous. Even now Regis Le Gwyn must be mobilis-
ing robots, ristos, nilskils — perhaps even teknos — but
he would not begin the hunt until the Lady Somavalt
was free. He would not wish to have it said that he allowed
a risto to die because he could not contain his anger.

Throughout the journey, Berry kept his pistol pointed
at Somavalt. One never knew with a woman.

He glanced many times at the huddled, shrouded figure
of Vron. She was only half-conscious — the sedatives

she had been given seemed very strong — but she had recognised him in one of her wakeful moments.

"Berry ... Berry ... You came for me," she had mumbled.

"Yes, I came for you. Do not worry. Rest."

After a time, Somavalt, still white-faced and shaken, plucked up the courage to speak. "Do you intend to kill me, savage, when I am of no further use?"

Berry looked shocked. "Let Regis Le Gwyn keep his word. I will keep mine. We of Earth are not animals. You ristos have much to learn."

"Where are you taking me?"

"Is it not obvious? The car is programmed for Parkzone. I am a man of the forest, hardened to its ways. Whatever Regis Le Gwyn may think, he is a man softened by easy living. When we meet again, I shall have the advantage."

The Lady Somavalt managed a faint smile. "Savage, you are a fool. The Controller will have twenty robots reprogrammed for homicide. They will search Parkzone until they find you. They will be well armed and they do not tire. What can you do against them?"

Berry shrugged. "To be both a savage and a fool may be advantageous. If we are hunted by robots, we will do what we can. At the very least, it will show all who live in Heaven Seven that your chief lacks the courage to face a dirtside foolish savage. But I think you are wrong, Lady. Regis Le Gwyn is a proud man. He will come to seek me."

"So will the robots."

"I have recently become an expert at disabling robots. Also, they are more vulnerable than men."

"Why do you say that?"

"Because, Lady, not being alive, they lack the will to

live . . . But, see, we have already arrived at the perimeter of Parkzone. This, I think, is Entrance Five."

The air-car stopped in front of the entrance. Berry lifted Vron gently out of the car and laid her on a grassy mound. She opened her eyes, murmured his name, then closed them again. He looked back towards Citizone. The nearest buildings were some distance away. It would take the Lady Somavalt several minutes to get to a V-phone. But, with Vron in her present condition, he needed more than a few minutes. While he contemplated the problem, he took the weapons he had acquired in Faczone out of the car.

He turned to Tala. "Have you any cord or rope?"

"No, Berry."

"So. It does not matter."

Somavalt gained courage. "You said you would release me now. Am I free to go?"

"I will do better," said Berry. "I will return you to Regis Le Gwyn. Please take off your gown."

"I will not!"

Berry threw himself upon her, tearing at the gown. "When the Night Comers take our women," he said, "they drag them by the feet. Think yourself lucky that you have to deal with a civilised man."

He began to tear the gown from her body. Somavalt struggled with amazing strength. In the end, he had to knock her head on the side of the air-car until her eyes clouded and she uttered a great sigh.

Tala watched him with amazement. "This is no time to revenge yourself by possessing a risto, Berry."

"Woman, try to think clearly," he said. "I keep my word. No harm shall come to this risto. Tear the gown into strips. We will bind her hands and her feet, and seal her mouth. Then I will programme the car to take her back to Regis Le Gwyn like a trussed fowl ready for the cooking. This will gain us time. Vron is in no condition to travel. I shall have to carry her." He grinned. "Also, I think, the temper of the Controller will not be improved when he sees how I have treated a female risto."

Tala tore some thin strips from the gown; then, with some strange sense of propriety, she put what was left of it back on the still dazed risto. The Lady Somavalt struggled feebly, but Berry managed to tie her wrists together and then her ankles. Then he bound another piece of the gown round her face and over her mouth. He laid her in the bottom of the air-car. If, despite the darkness, anyone noticed that the car was apparently empty as it passed through Citizone, no doubt they would think it had been programmed to collect a late reveller.

Finally, Berry reset the keys on the programme panel. He had remembered the code: CA10-27. He set the car for fast drive and pressed the go key.

The car lifted.

"Farewell, Lady Somavalt," called Berry. "Live long. Get many children — but not from proxy wombs."

The air-car swung back towards Citizone.

One thing that Berry had omitted to take from the Commissariat was a hand lamp. He was thankful now for the illusion of starlight and moonlight. If the night had been a dark one, as he had hoped earlier, he would have experienced some difficulty.

Parkzone was separated from the rest of Heaven Seven by a barrier consisting of three thicknesses of plastiglass, the spaces between the plastiglass panels being evacuated to eliminate heat exchange. The barrier rose from ground level to the dome. It was a miracle of engineering. Berry marvelled at it. His crash course in the sciences enabled him to appreciate the theory and also the immense difficulties of construction.

On both sides of the axis of Heaven Seven there were

five entrances to Parkzone. Each of the entrances consisted of wide, air-sealed revolving doors that could only be activated by the presentation of an authorisation disc. Berry did not have an authorisation disc; but that was not a serious problem, he thought. He could use his hunting laser to short the electronic lock or, if that did not work, he could simply burn through the barrier. There was a slight difference in air pressure between Parkzone and the rest of Heaven Seven — necessary, chiefly, to maintain the stability of the barrier which, though it looked solid enough, was flexible because of its sheer size. In effect, the barrier was a vast skin, made firm as the skin of a balloon is made firm by internal pressure.

However, if Berry were forced to puncture the skin, it was almost certain that service robots would repair the damage before the barrier began to flap and rupture itself. In any case, he reflected, he had no cause to be overly concerned about possible hazards to the inhabitants of Heaven Seven. They had exploited the people and the resources of Earth for many centuries. Their chief virtue was that they had maintained and increased the ancient knowledge. Also they had developed many skills that could be useful to the people of Earth. If only those skills could be passed on to the clans . . .

He stopped this train of thought and came back to practicalities. He saw that Tala was attending to Vron.

"How is she?"

"She has times of wakefulness. Her mind is clearing, but slowly. She is very weak."

"I shall have to carry her, then. You will have to carry all our weapons. Can you do that?"

"Yes, my chief. I can do it."

"Good. We have little time. By now, the Lady Somavalt will be half way to her destination. The moment she speaks to Regis Le Gwyn, robots will be programmed to trace our flight. I am now going to force an entry into Parkzone. Be ready. It will not take long."

Berry examined the mechanism of the revolving doors. He cursed the lack of a hand lamp. He could not see where the locking circuits lay. In desperation, he lasered all round the panel which accepted the authorisation discs. Still the doors would not move. Finally, he decided to cut a hole through the barrier.

The plastiglass melted rapidly. Soon he had cut a tunnel through the three membranes. It was not a big hole. But it was big enough for a man to crawl through it on his hands and knees.

"How is she?"

"Sleeping once more, Berry."

"Perhaps it is as well ... I will go through first. Pass the weapons to me. Then drag Vron so that I may hold her arms and pull her through. You will follow. Can you do this?"

"I can do it."

The air rushed out of Parkzone with greater force than Berry had anticipated. He crawled through the gap, feeling the warm winds on his body, exhilarated by the subtle scents of the forest borne on them.

"Pass the weapons through," he called.

Afterwards, and with some difficulty, Tala moved Vron, half-awake and protesting sleepily, so that Berry could stretch through the tunnel and take hold of her arms. He hauled her gently through the gap. Tala followed. The air of Parkzone continued to rush noisily through the hole.

"Now," said Berry. "Listen carefully. I studied the lay-out of Parkzone as part of my orientation programme. The part we have entered corresponds most closely with the forests that I knew on Earth. We must find somewhere to rest safely until daylight comes. By then, let us hope, Vron will be sufficiently recovered to walk. If she is not, I will have to carry her.

"Meanwhile, if I am not mistaken, Regis Le Gwyn will send robots to find us. They can see in the dark better than we can, also they do not tire. These are their advantages. But they move noisily and clumsily, as you must know, also they do not know the lore of the forest. These are our advantages. We will seek a place as far as we can get from this hole in the barrier. There we will rest until first light. Come now. Gather our weapons, and handle this laser carefully. This is the safety stud. I have pressed it. If you do not touch it, the weapon cannot discharge."

Tala began to gather up the weapons. She looked at the shadowy trees and could not repress a shudder. "The robots will find us before morning," she said gloomily. "Then they will kill us or take us back to the Controller so that he may devise a worse fate."

"The robots may find us," conceded Berry. "But they will not kill us, nor will they take us to the Controller."

"How do you know this?"

"Because Regis Le Gwyn is a very proud and a very angry man. Doubtless he will let the robots pinpoint us. But he will wish to do the hunting himself. I am a dirt-side animal, he is a Heavenside risto. He will need to prove to his people and, perhaps, to himself that he is superior in every way. He will come. He will bring fellow ristos — heavily armed, I expect — to witness his triumph. But he will come."

"Will you try to kill him?" asked Tala. "It would at least give some satisfaction to know that he accompanied us into the everlasting dark."

"There are times when it is wiser not to kill," said

Berry enigmatically. "But we shall see." He stooped, lifted Vron and laid her over his shoulder. She grunted somewhat and called his name. He paid no attention. "We will not enter the forest from here," he said. "It is too obvious. Let us follow the barrier for a while. When we begin to tire, we will enter the forest."

Twenty-two

VRON WAS A PLUMP and heavy woman. Slowly, agonisingly, Berry managed to carry her perhaps half a kilometre away from the barrier before he realised he could carry her no more. He was exhausted. He would have to rest and regain his strength, otherwise he would be useless for any confrontation with robots or ristos.

During the short and gruelling journey, Vron had regained consciousness several times. On one of these occasions Berry had tried to get her to stand; but her legs had buckled and she sank to her knees.

Not far from where Berry himself collapsed under the strain of carrying a woman almost as heavy as he was, there ran a stream narrow enough for a man to stride over. Berry, unable to speak, motioned to Tala. She put the weapons down then helped him to drag Vron to the edge of the stream. While Berry rested, somewhat fearful that his heart might burst, Tala splashed Vron's face repeatedly with cool water.

Vron moaned and shivered, and coughed and grunted and uttered much nonsense like one drunk. But, suddenly, her wits and her strength seemed to return.

She sat up, gazed intently at Berry as if to assure herself that he was real, then looked at Tala.

"Who is this woman? Is she a tekno bitch? How did you get here? Why are you wearing a tekno robe, Berry? Where are we?"

"Be quiet, Vron!" snapped Berry irritably. "You were

less trouble when you were senseless. There are questions enough in my mind without you adding to them. Our lives are in danger, and I must think carefully. Will you be quiet or shall I knock you on the head?"

"I am sorry, Berry." Vron's eyes filled with tears. "I am very confused. These people did strange things to me. They took away the child I would have borne for you. I tried not to let them. But the tekno women were strong and I was weak. Also they pricked my arm many times and destroyed my will, making me wish only to sleep. It is enough that you have found me. I will be quiet."

Berry was ashamed at his outburst. He stretched out a hand and held Vron's breast, as he used to do on Earth when he wished to show affection or lie with her.

"I, too, am sorry. My words were harsh because much depends on what we do next. I will answer your questions as quickly as I may, but first I must ask you a question. Can you now walk?"

Vron gave a sigh. "My strength returns, I think. I can walk." She gave a bitter laugh. "Any woman of the Londos who is not mortally wounded can walk. Is that not so?"

"Indeed it is. We are a peaceful people, but strong. Now listen carefully. This woman, Tala, is also now a woman of the Londos. She knows the ways of these Heavenside people, having been here for many seasons. She will help us to return to the clan."

Then, quickly, he told her of all that had happened since the Night Comers had raided the Londos settlement, omitting nothing.

"So Tala is your woman also?" asked Vron, though it was more a statement than a question.

"We have lain together," said Berry. He smiled. "She may yet bear my child."

"Then I will love her," said Vron simply, "because she has given you pleasure." She held out her hand to Tala. The two women kissed.

"Since you can walk," said Berry, "we will cross this stream and go into the forest until you are too tired to walk farther. There we will rest and wait for daylight." He laughed grimly. "Or for the robots of Regis Le Gwyn."

Vron travelled farther and longer than Berry had dared to hope. The trees of the forest were not as tall or as densely growing as in the forests Berry knew. The moonlight made it easy to see where to step. Many times Berry called a halt, partly so that Vron might have a brief rest, but chiefly so that he could listen for sounds of pursuit. He heard none, and was a little puzzled. It was impossible that the gap in the barrier had not yet been discovered. Perhaps Regis Le Gwyn was delaying the pursuit until daylight, when he himself might take part.

Berry kept close to the stream, travelling up it. Food he already had; but it was as well to stay close to water. Now and again, he glanced up at the moon and the stars, finding it hard to believe that they were not real but simply projections of light on the dome of Heaven Seven. The stars were already beginning to fade from the sky, indicating the approach of morning, when Vron confessed that she could walk no longer.

They had reached a patch of high ground on the top of which there was a softy grassy hollow. It seemed a comfortable place to rest. The surrounding trees were thicker than in other parts of the forest, and the tiny stream ran almost half way round the small hump of ground.

"You have done well," Berry told Vron. "We will eat, drink and rest now. Later, we shall need much strength."

He opened a pack of the food concentrates. They were

large tablets that could be bitten and chewed. They had an unidentifiable but pleasant taste. Washed down with water from the stream, they gave a feeling of repletion. In the pack of concentrates there was also a small box containing a number of tiny translucent red spheres no larger than holly berries. Presumably, they also were for eating. Experimentally, Berry chewed one. It had a very sweet taste and rapidly dissolved in his mouth.

After a time, his vision blurred and there was a roaring in his ears. He began to regret his recklessness. But presently his eyes cleared, the noise in his ears faded, and he felt a pleasant tingling in his feet and hands. Most important of all, he no longer ached with the strain of carrying Vron, and he no longer felt weary. Also, his mind seemed wonderfully clear.

"Bors Zangwin has provided us with something that may be even more valuable than food." He gave one of the capsules to each of the women. "Eat it. There will be some unpleasant feelings, but they will pass. Then you will no longer feel tired. It is some kind of neural stimulant. Most powerful in its effect."

Vron looked at the tiny sphere doubtfully. "You are sure it is not poison?"

Berry smiled. "I am sure. The Programmer would not use all the skills of the teknos to fashion an arrow and then deliberately blunt its point."

When he saw that the two women had passed through the unpleasant side-effects and were receiving the benefit of the stimulant, he explained part of his plan to them. He did not tell them all of it because he knew they would have thought him mad.

"We will be hunted," he said calmly, "if, indeed, the hunt has not already begun. We will be hunted as animals because most of the people of Heaven Seven regard us as animals. If they can, they will kill us as we of Earth would kill deer. But whereas we of Earth would kill only for food, these people would kill for sport.

"Regis Le Gwyn may send robots and homing bees to seek us out. Indeed, I believe he will. But I gamble on the man's pride. He, the chief of his people, has been defied and humiliated by a dirtside savage. If I read him aright — and I think I am a judge of men — he will wish to make the kill himself. He will wish to redeem himself in his own eyes and in the eyes of his clan, the ristos."

"What are homing bees?" asked Vron.

Berry sighed. How could he explain the intricacies of micro-miniaturised guidance systems to Vron, who knew how to roast venison to perfection and how to give much pleasure to a man but had no knowledge of basic science?

"They are machines, as the robots are machines. They are small and they can transport themselves through the air. They can be made to seek out objects, animals or people."

Vron shivered. "Then we cannot escape. We shall be found, and they will kill us. Still not to have to die alone is something."

"Woman," said Berry furiously, "I have already had much talk of dying from Tala. Let there be an end to it. These people of Heaven Seven have great skills, and machines to serve them. But their spirits have not been hardened as ours have been hardened by the cruel ways of nature. They have not had to make their life in the forest. They have not had to hunt their food and starve if they could not find it. They have not had to fight for their very existence as we have had to fight. They are clever, yes. But they are also weak. Weak and proud. Therefore they are vulnerable. The stoat is smaller than the rabbit, and less powerful. But the stoat is a hunter and the rabbit is not. We are dealing with rabbits who presume to be hunters. Let them come ... Now, you and Tala will rest while I keep watch. When you have rested, we will move from this place and I will choose a point where we may wait for our pursuers. They will not relish the encounter, I promise you."

"My chief," said Vron, "if we kill the hunters, more will surely come. What then?"

"It is simple," said Berry. "We will destroy the whole of Heaven Seven, and all who live here, or we will return freely to Earth. Now rest."

"Chief," said Tala, "there is greatness or madness in your mind. I do not know which."

Berry laughed. "Nor do I. But the day will reveal."

Twenty-three

A HOMING BEE CAME buzzing through the forest shortly after daybreak. At first, it did not come near Berry's little camp but seemed to jerk about aimlessly among the trees on the other side of the small stream. Then it buzzed away. Berry thought that it would not be long before it returned. He was right.

He had allowed the women to doze while he kept watch. Vron managed to relax, but Tala tossed restlessly. The effect of the neural stimulant had not diminished, and her awareness of physical fatigue was minimal. Berry was under no illusion about the value of the drug they had taken. It could not create energy. It could only make the brain ignore bodily tiredness. It was useful but dangerous. It would enable a man or a woman to exert themselves to the fullest until they dropped.

When the homing bee came back, he was ready for it. He knew all about homing bees. They were intricate mechanisms, almost spherical in shape and about the size of a man's head. They operated on sonic, visual and heat-sensing systems; and their propulsion engines — which made the buzzing sound — were powered by tiny nuclear-fuelled jet engines. They had been designed entirely for use in Parkzone, to seek out people who were lost or in difficulty and to seek out mammalian targets for hunting parties. He guessed that homing bees would be used to act as seekers for the clumsy and noisy robots. When the quarry was found, the bee would signal to the robots. They would doubtless then close in, ensure that escape would be impossible, and wait for the ristos to come and demonstrate their superiority over three rebellious savages. Such, reasoned Berry, would be the strategy of Regis Le Gwyn. He was not the kind of man who would wish to do any of the hard work himself, or take risks. Therefore he would wait until the savages were pinned down. Then he would display his bravery.

But why had he waited so long? Berry knew that the technological facilities of Heaven Seven were such that the bees and the robots could have found the escaped slaves hours ago, in the middle of the night. Why had the Controller of Heaven Seven waited until daybreak? Was it simply that he required a good night's sleep before he took his revenge? Bearing in mind the temperament of the Controller, that hardly seemed likely.

Suddenly Berry knew why Regis Le Gwyn had delayed the pursuit. He wanted the final confrontation to be in broad daylight. He wanted this not only because it would be to his advantage as the hunter but also because the sequence of events could be clearly relayed to the V-screens of Citizone. It was not enough that the dirtside savages should be destroyed. The method of their destruction must be witnessed by the people who had elected the Controller to power.

When the homing bee came back, Berry allowed it to register his position clearly, then he lasered it. The bee exploded with a flash in mid-air. Tala sat up instantly. Vron was slower to return to full consciousness.

"I gave the bee time to recognise us and relay our position," he said calmly. "Soon, I think, the robots will come."

Vron said: "Then we must run, Berry. It is good that I now feel strong."

Berry took off his tekno robe and stood only in his

short tunic. It was good to feel the morning air on his skin. "No. I will go. You will stay."

Tala looked at him in sorrow. "You would now desert us, my chief. It is well. By yourself, you will live longer."

"Woman, use your wits," he said roughly. "I go to hunt the hunters. Make the tekno robe look as if a body lies inside it. If the robots come, as I believe, shout at them, plead with them, make much noise. You understand?"

"I understand. Forgive me, chief."

"Only do as I say," snapped Berry.

There were heavy noises in the forest. They were still distant but seemed to be on all sides.

Berry smiled. "The machines oblige us greatly by advertising their intentions." He took up the hunting laser. "I will go now."

"Will the robots not put us to sleep as they did on Earth?" asked Vron.

"If they do, all is lost and I have entirely misjudged Regis Le Gwyn. But I believe the man wants sport as well as revenge. It will give him greater satisfaction to hunt us than to have our unconscious bodies laid at his feet."

"Good hunting to you, Berry."

"Thank you. Now make the robe look somewhat like a fallen man. Hurry!"

Twenty-four

BERRY HAD CLIMBED A tall hardwood tree not far from the grassy mound where Vron and Tala remained. He had a clear view of the knoll. He could see that the discarded tekno robe looked as if it might contain the shape of a man. He had watched Vron and Tala hastily stuffing the sleeves and hood with handfuls of grass. Tala had taken off her own robe and rumpled it up to lend substance to the body.

Three robots had now arrived on the scene. Berry was relieved to see that they were not armed and that though they carried gas cylinders they showed no inclination to use them. They stood well back from the grassy mound. No doubt, as Berry had anticipated, they were instructed only to keep the savages pinned down until the Controller arrived.

The robots, aware that the savages possessed at least one hunting laser, each stood near a tree behind which it might take cover if necessary. Berry hoped that, when he attacked them, it would take valuable seconds for them to discover that the attack was from the rear, and more valuable seconds to discover precisely where. Machines such as these he already knew could react faster than human beings. He would need both time and luck if he were to knock them all out.

The two women were following their instructions and making a lot of noise. Tala appeared to be trying to engage the robots in conversation and, judging from her gestures, pleading with them. One of the robots answered her; but Berry could not hear the words which passed between them. Nevertheless, he judged that the distraction would be of much help.

He waited for a time to see if any more robots were on their way. The forest remained quiet, except for the noises of birds and the quick, startling passage of a young deer. It would have been so easy to laser the deer; and Berry reflected briefly how much easier the life of the clans would be if they had weapons such as he now possessed. How much more bloody also, he reflected, would be the clan wars. The power of the laser in the hands of a wise man would be a good thing; but in the hands of a fool it would be devastating.

Presently, satisfied that three robots only had been instructed to pin down or follow the dirtside savages, Berry decided that he could wait no longer. Even now, a party of ristos would be on their way.

He set the hunting laser for maximum power. He begrudged such a massive use of energy, since the micropile indicator told him that nearly a quarter of the energy reserve had already been discharged. But he could not afford to take any risks.

Tala was still haranguing the robots hysterically or with feigned hysteria. Their attention seemed to be concentrated wholly on the grassy mound.

Berry sighted carefully, squeezed the discharge button. One robot's headpiece glowed red, and vapour came from the laser hole. It fell over, threshing about. The two remaining robots gazed at it, then turned to scan behind them. As they turned, a second robot received the full laser discharge. The last robot, being unable to determine where the attack came from, began to retreat swiftly. Berry still aimed for the headpiece; but the robot was very fast, and he only succeeded in disabling the motor mechanism of the legs. The robot fell, but continued to haul itself away, using its powerful arms. Berry burned it again and again until it lay still.

Then he climbed quickly down the tree and finished off the two robots which still probably had functioning communication relays.

"That was well done," called Tala. "I was afraid they would use the gas."

"It took much laser energy," said Berry. "Fortunately, our pursuers do not know that we have only one such weapon. Hurry, now. We must be away from here very quickly. Give Vron the anaesthetic gun. It is simple to use. I will show her. You, Tala, take the crossbow, the bolts and the hunting knife. I will carry the javelins and the hatchet." Regretfully, he put on the tekno robe once more. It had useful pockets which would enable him to carry the transceiver and the food concentrate.

Soon they were ready to move.

"Where must be go, Berry?" asked Vron. "Do you know where we can be safe?"

"We cannot be safe while Regis Le Gwyn hunts us," said Berry. "I want to go towards the axis," he added obscurely, "but at present we cannot do that. It would seem too obvious. We must try to make our pursuers believe that our moves are random or foolish. Therefore we will move towards the perimeter. When we have travelled a few kilometres, we will find another suitable place to rest.

"What is a kilometre?"

"A distance about six times the length of an arrow's full flight," he answered impatiently. "Come, now. I will explain more when we have found some safer place."

Twenty-five

BY MID-MORNING BERRY HAD found a suitable temporary refuge at the edge of a small, shallow lake. On the far side of the lake there was grassland, supporting shrubs and bushes, and the nearest trees were more than a hundred metres from the edge of the lake. On the side he had chosen there was a rocky overhang below which it would be possible for him and the two women to conceal themselves completely, and on top of which there were tall luxuriant grasses also capable of providing concealment.

It was an excellent place to lie low. Human beings or robots searching the area would have great difficulty finding the fugitives until and unless they were almost literally on top of them. The chief danger was from machines such as the homing bees that could detect bodily heat.

The air was much warmer by the lake, not only because the synthetic sun had risen but also because, as Berry knew, they were now near to the tropical area of Parkzone.

Though Vron had uttered no complaint, the journey had fatigued her despite the earlier boost given by the stimulant. As they rested Berry explained to the women what he had learned about Heaven Seven, and Parkzone in particular, during the intensive education programme devised by Bors Zangwin.

"Heaven Seven is roughly in the shape of a compressed

sphere about twenty kilometres in diameter," he began.

"Please, Berry, make this more clear so that I may properly understand," pleaded Vron.

He sighed. He had learned so much during his stay in Faczone that he now found it difficult to comprehend how ignorant he had previously been. But Vron, who had been in Heaven Seven but a little time, knew nothing of its structure. Even Tala, who had been here long enough to bear three babies, understood little of the function and magnitude of the vast orbiting satellite to which they had been brought.

"Think of a bubble," he said at last. "When a baby has taken much milk at the breast, it also swallows air. And when it is satisfied it brings up the air. If the baby's lips are closed and if there is still much milk upon them, the air is trapped in a bubble, the skin of which is the mother's milk . . . I have seen this thing, Vron. I have seen it many times when you fed little Vron. You remember also?"

"I remember."

"The milk bubble bursts quickly. But think of a bubble that does not burst. Think of a bubble that can be squeezed so that it is no longer like a ball in shape but like a smooth, rounded stone, such as you might find by the sea. Heaven Seven is a bubble of such a shape. It has a skin which protects us from the cold emptiness of space. On the inside surface of this skin are projected the illusions of the sky, the sun, the moon, the stars. Tala already knows, for she has told me, how Heaven Seven was expanded over hundreds of years by absorbing smaller satellites, cosmic debris and materials from Earth.

"This vast flattened bubble, Vron, is as wide as a man may march in a full day — twenty kilometres. I have told you what a kilometre is. Can you remember?"

Vron thought for a moment. "A distance of about six arrow flights?"

"Good. It follows that if the diameter of Heaven Seven is twenty kilometres, its inside plane area — using the simple formula πr^2 — must be approximately three hundred and fourteen square kilometres. Of this area about two thirds — let us say two hundred square kilometres — are given over to Parkzone. The rest is divided between Faczone and Citizone. So — "

"Berry, please!" Tala held her head. "You use words I don't understand, you make me dizzy."

"You are right. Sufficient for you to know, Tala, that Parkzone is big enough to enable us to hide for some time, if we are careful. Also, it contains many different kinds of forest land where strange animals abound, some of them very dangerous.

"But do not believe that we can only be trapped here as the animals are trapped. We shall escape."

"What escape is there from Heaven Seven?" demanded Tala. "The flattened bubble, as you have called it, is only a large cage."

Berry smiled. "The cage has a door. I have little time to tell you about it now, but I will say this: think of the flattened bubble and imagine a tube that passes through its centre. Part of that tube is the satellite's dock, the place where its space vessel enters and departs. The dock can be entered from Parkzone as well as from Faczone and Citizone. Now do you understand?"

"Can you fly a space vessel, Berry?"

"I have learned much. I can try. But that is not important. It is more important that we gain possession of the vessel. Without it, the people of Heaven Seven — ristos, teknos and nilskils alike — will be destroyed."

"Why is that?"

"Because they need the women of Earth to breed new

generations. Because they suffer too much genetic damage from hard radiation. Heaven Seven is their cage as well as ours. Caged animals do not live for ever. Now do you understand?"

"Chief," said Tala, "you are a great man."

Berry sighed. "I am a man pressed for time, an impatient man. Now listen carefully. Where we now rest is a good hiding place, hard to discover. I am leaving you for a time, but I will return presently. I will take with me the crossbow and the quiver of bolts, leaving you the hunting laser, the anaesthetic gun, the hatchet, knife and javelins. I have shown you how to use the laser and the anagun. The greatest danger at present, I think, is from homing bees. If you see one laser it instantly. If robots come, do nothing unless you are sure they are aware of your presence. If they discover you, laser their vision circuits and then their communication circuits, as you have seen me do. If ristos come — which is unlikely — use the anagun. But if you are hard pressed use the laser."

"It will be as you command."

Berry took off his tekno robe and removed the transceiver from its pocket. Then he picked up the crossbow and the quiver of bolts.

"Berry, where are you going?" asked Vron. "What do you wish to do?"

"I go to press a thorn into the hide of Regis Le Gwyn," he answered. He touched the transceiver. "This is my thorn and, because its position can be traced, I must be some kilometres away from our resting place before I can use it. Do not fret, Vron. I will return before the sun is high."

"But if you do not return, my chief?" enquired Tala calmly.

"Use the hunting laser," said Berry. "It is swift and there will be little pain."

143

Twenty-six

BERRY PLACED THE TRANSCEIVER on a small rock, sat
down and waited until he had stopped sweating and his
breathing had returned to normal. He estimated that he
had run about five kilometres. Before he had left the
women, he had swallowed another of the tiny, translucent
red spheres that eliminated awareness of fatigue and
produced the illusion of abundant reserves of energy. He
wondered how long it would be before such stimulants
proved useless. At the very least, there were many hours
of strenuous activity before him; and he would need
to be at maximum alertness. Time was on the side of
Regis Le Gwyn.

The transceiver was a versatile instrument — a miracle
of micro circuitry which Berry's recently acquired knowledge of electronics allowed him to appreciate. It could
be used simply as a radiotelephone or V-phone, or as an
all channels receiver or an all channels transmitter. If the
distress circuit were used, it would broadcast on maximum
power simultaneously on all channels.

When he had recovered from his exertions, Berry
pressed the T stud.

A mechanical voice said: "Comcentre. Whom do you
wish to contact?"

"Regis Le Gwyn."

"Vision and sound, or sound only?"

"Vision and sound."

"Engage the V circuit, please, and stand by. If person called declines to accept, do you wish to identify?"

"Person called will accept," said Berry. "Tell him the caller is a dirtside savage."

After a few moments, the V screen revealed the head and shoulders of Regis Le Gwyn. Berry tried to discern the background; but it was fuzzy and he could not determine if the Controller was in Citizone or Parkzone.

"Well, savage," said Regis Le Gwyn, "I trust you enjoyed your night of mischief. You will pay for it dearly. I hope you are not about to bore me by pleading for mercy. In a very short time you will wish that you had never been born."

Berry moved himself close to the transceiver's lens, thus blotting out his own background.

"Chief, I called to enquire if the Lady Somavalt is alive and well. Also, I wondered if, having had time for thought, you would be prepared to negotiate terms. I am a reasonable man."

Regis Le Gwyn laughed. "You are a reasonable man! That is funny. That is very funny. I will savour the humour of it as I watch you die slowly. But, for your information, savage, the Lady Somavalt is alive and well. Since she suffered some indignity at your hands, I have invited her to witness your destruction."

"Have care, chief, that she does not witness your own destruction."

"I am coming for you, Berry."

Berry smiled. "Then I shall not be disappointed. It is a good day for a hunt. Chief, you are a stupid man. Farewell until we meet." He cut the transmission, knowing that direction-finders would have already pinpointed his exact location and that homing bees and robots would already be on their way.

There was not much time left, but perhaps there was

enough. He pressed the Distress stud, thus ensuring that his next broadcast would be on all channels at maximum strength, and automatically relayed by the Communications Centre in Faczone.

"To the people of Heaven Seven, from Berry, chief of the Londos tribe on Earth, greetings. Your Controller has sworn to kill me. I await his coming. He calls me a dirtside savage, and thinks himself a better man. Thus far, this dirtside savage has disabled many robots and a homing bee. Doubtless more will be sent against me. I have two companions. If the Controller truly believes that ristos are superior to dirtside savages, let him also come against me with two companions. If he needs more, he will have already shown that he is weak and unfit to be chief of his clan. That is all I have to say."

Berry switched off the transceiver then took a deep breath and prepared to run back to the place where he had left Tala and Vron.

He felt he had done the best he could. He had goaded Regis Le Gwyn privately and publicly. If he had judged the nature of the Controller correctly, Regis Le Gwyn would respond to the challenge. Robots and bees would doubtless be used to track down the quarry; but they would not be programmed for offensive action. The Controller would be proud enough and angry enough to wish to destroy the dirtside savages himself. And therein lay his weakness.

Twenty-seven

BERRY RETURNED TO THE lake with far greater care than when he had left it. Though he ran swiftly, every few hundred metres he stopped, hid himself and listened. If any robots or bees were in the vicinity when he used the transceiver, the d/f station would have given them his exact position. He did not harbour any illusions about the efficiency of robots and bees. So long as their micropiles operated, they could travel far faster than he could. They did not need stimulants and they did not get tired.

But luck, apparently, was with him. He detected no signs of pursuit.

"Did you push your thorn into the flesh of the Controller?" asked Tala.

Berry smiled. "I did. We shall not have to wait long. Has anything happened in my absence?"

"One of the homing bees came," said Vron. "Tala destroyed it as you commanded."

"Good. Did it have time to observe?"

"No, chief," said Tala. "These things are very noisy. We were aware of its coming and were ready before we saw it. I was able to beam it down as soon as it came into view."

"You did well. Its destruction will be noted, and the point where it was destroyed will be noted. More will follow, but they must not be destroyed, for they will be the eyes and ears of the people of Heaven Seven. They will witness my encounter with Regis Le Gwyn."

"Berry," said Vron, "would it not be wise to go from this place, hoping that we will not be found?"

He shook his head. "We shall be found, sooner or later. Better that it be sooner, and at a time and place of my choosing. I choose this place. There are trout in the lake, I see. I have a mind to taste the flesh of trout once more. I will take two out of the shallows, then I will make a wood fire and cook them and eat them. It will give me much pleasure."

"But the smoke from the fire!" protested Vron. "It will be a signal of your presence."

"It is meant to be," said Berry. "You and Tala will hide yourselves in the long grasses on the far side of this pool. If robots come, you will pay no attention. Above all, you will remain concealed. If homing bees come, you will ignore them unless they detect your presence. In which case you will laser them. But I think the heat of my fire will distract them from the heat of your bodies. Presently, I think, Regis Le Gwyn will come, probably with two or more human companions. I shall do my best to remain unaware of his arrival." He grinned. "In any case, I shall have only the crossbow to defend myself. I think it will be a poor defence against three or more hunting lasers."

"You wish to be taken?" demanded Tala, her eyes wide.

"No. If you see that I am about to be killed, you will do your best to laser or anaesthetise all who attack me. But if I am allowed to talk — as I think may be the case — you will do nothing unless you hear me use the words 'dirtside savages'. Then you, Tala, will laser all the Controller's companions, if you can. And you, Vron, will put an anaesthetic dart into the Controller himself. Unless I am killed, it is important that he does not die. Do you understand?"

"We understand," said Tala. "Chief, we have little

knowledge of these strange weapons. You will trust us?"

"It is necessary that I trust you. There is little time. Take some practice shots, then go round the lake and conceal yourselves. You will hear my voice. I will speak loud."

While the women practised briefly with their weapons — not wishing to use too many anaesthetic darts or too much of the hunting laser's power — Berry took two of his javelins and stood on the rocky overhang by the side of the lake. He gazed down at the water, and sighed. It was an attractive pool. If only it were a pool in the forests he knew on Earth! He would have been content to spend the entire morning spearing trout.

Vron tossed a few large pebbles into the air. Tala lasered them — or most of them. Her aim was good for a woman unused to such a weapon. Then it was her turn to fling targets while Vron tried to hit them with darts from the anagun. She was less successful. But Berry, watching out of the corner of his eyes, was content. He knew that the anagun was the more difficult weapon. Its darts took far longer to find their target than the light-speed beam of the laser.

Presently two fat trout idled into the shallows. Berry transfixed one, but missed the other. He scrambled down the rock and waded into the water to retrieve his javelins and the fish. He rejoiced in the feel of the cold water around his legs.

The trout he had taken was a big one. He would not need another.

Tala had already collected enough twigs for a fire. She piled them together skilfully. "You will make the flame yourself?" she asked.

Berry shook his head. "Here we have little time, and greater convenience. Laser the twigs for me. Then go quickly. When the smoke rises, we will not have to wait long."

Presently, Vron and Tala had concealed themselves on the far side of the small lake. Berry gazed carefully at the far bank. He could not see them, and was satisfied. Tranquilly, he began to cook the trout he had taken. It smelled good.

Presently, he heard the sound of a homing bee, then of another. Then of a third. The bees hovered in the air, their electronic heat sensors drawn by the fire. Berry piled more wood upon it, hoping that the sophisticated mechanisms would not also register the bodily heat of the two women on the far side of the lake.

Presently, while Berry cooked his trout to perfection, he heard the sound of men approaching. They moved through the forest more quietly than robots. He did not look up until they were close behind him, and until Regis Le Gwyn spoke.

Twenty-eight

"WHERE ARE THE FEMALES?" Regis Le Gwyn held a large capacity hunting laser, and it was pointed unerringly at Berry's head. He had two risto companions. They also carried heavy hunting lasers. They paid no attention to Berry but peered intently at the tall grasses, the bushes and the nearer trees. Berry saw that they were very nervous, ready to laser anything that moved.

Berry made as if to reach for his crossbow, which was already charged with a bolt. Regis Le Gwyn lasered it instantly, reducing it to a charred and useless wreck. Then he swung the laser back to point at Berry. "Where are the women? Speak savage. You are about to die, but the manner of your death is in my hands."

Berry shrugged. "Chief, they were much afraid. It is a great disappointment, but one that I must bear. Who can tell what women will do when they are angry or afraid? Thinking myself cunning, I left them while I went to another place to use the transceiver, knowing that you would pinpoint my broadcast. When I returned, they were gone ... It was a mistake to leave them ... I did not expect you so soon, chief. Doubtless you know the ways of the forest better than I had thought. It is a matter for regret."

Regis Le Gwyn laughed. "It is indeed a matter for regret. But be consoled, Nothing-but-Berry. Your regret will not last long."

The homing bees, Berry was relieved to see, drew

closer to the fire and the men who confronted him. Evidently the heat of the fire and the bodies of four men was enough to temporarily distract their sensing mechanism from further investigation.

Berry looked at the trout he had been cooking. "I am very hungry, chief, having had nothing to eat for a long time. It is said that a man dies well on a full stomach. Will you permit me to eat?"

"Savage," said Regis Le Gwyn, glancing at the hovering bees, "you have caused much trouble, but we of Heaven Seven are not animals such as you. We are civilised. Eat your fish, if it will give you some satisfaction. You have already paid for it dearly. If you had not lighted a fire, doubtless we should have taken longer to track you down . . . That is the difference between the civilised man and the animals. The animal thinks chiefly of food."

"Thank you, chief," said Berry humbly. He took the trout from the forked stick he had used to cook it, skilfully peeled back the skin and began to gnaw avidly at the white flesh.

Regis Le Gwyn lowered his laser and glanced at his companions. "Are there any signs of the females?"

"None, Controller. It seems they have left this part of Parkzone."

"No matter. They will be found. We have here the prime mover. There will be no more trouble when he is dead."

Berry glanced up at the homing bees. "They are very cunning mechanisms, chief. Is it true that they can pass on the knowledge of what is happening here?"

"Savage, I do not know what the teknos have taught you, or why the Programmer saw fit to give you dangerous knowledge. But I mean to have answers to these questions before you are punished for crimes committed against the people of Heaven Seven ... Yes, the bees are relaying what passes between us. My people have a right to see justice done."

"It is well," said Berry. "A clan should know the qualities of its chief. No doubt many of your people will be glad to witness my destruction ... Did you truly come against me with only two companions?"

Regis Le Gwyn smiled. "Were more needed? We ristos know how to hunt animals."

"I am sorry I did not give you better sport."

"Now, savage. Time runs short for you. What passed between you and Bors Zangwin? Did he allow you to escape in order to assassinate me?"

"Chief, you must know he did not," said Berry reasonably. "The Programmer tested my Q ratings. Apparently, the results encouraged him to devise further experiments. The teknos fed me well and offered no violence. For that I am grateful ... Also, chief, if I had wished to kill you, that could have been accomplished when I visited the home of the Lady Somavalt, could it not? Perhaps that was my first mistake."

Evidently the Controller did not wish to be reminded of what had passed between him and Berry at the home of the Lady Somavalt. "I have means of loosening your tongue, savage. Speak the truth or I will use them."

"Lord," said Berry servilely, "my life is in your hands. I speak the truth. I stole a laser and short-circuited the lock where I was imprisoned. Then I fled with Tala and came to the house of the Lady Somavalt. The rest you know."

"Where is the laser now?"

Berry shrugged. "Too late I have learned that one should never trust a woman — even of my own tribe."

"I think your animal mind is cunning, savage. Not intelligent, but cunning. I think you are still trying to deceive me. I will ask more questions. If I am not satisfied that you speak the truth, I will burn one eye from your head. Then I will ask again. If you still try to deceive me I will burn the other eye, and leave you here in Parkzone. Before you die, you will experience much pain and much fear."

Berry paled. "I had thought you to be a civilised man, Controller."

"I am. But I am not dealing with a civilised man. Now, the questions. Did Bors Zangwin give you the laser?"

"He did not."

"Did he tell you where it could be found?"

"Chief, the Programmer is a very intelligent but slightly careless man. He mentioned once that he possessed a hunting laser. I remembered the fact and discovered where he kept it."

"I ask again: did you enter into any plot or agreement with Bors Zangwin?"

"No, chief. I learned much from the teknos, but they made no demands of me." He gazed innocently at the Controller. "Are they not loyal members of your own clan?"

Regis Le Gwyn's voice became hard. "Tell me exactly what you learned from the teknos."

"I learned to play chess. It is an interesting game, Controller, as you must know. I was told that at your last encounter with the Programmer, he defeated you. Most interesting."

Regis Le Gwyn sighted his laser on Berry's left eye. "Why is that most interesting, animal?"

"Because, chief," said Berry, raising his voice, "I have defeated Bors Zangwin. Perhaps, now, you will revise your opinion of dirtside savages."

There was a great cry on the far side of the lake. Vron stood up, revealing herself.

The three ristos half-turned. The Controller's two companions were lasered as they did so.

Regis Le Gwyn swung his hunting laser towards Vron. Berry dived at his feet, bringing him down. The anaesthetic dart whistled past, missing its target. Berry flung himself on top of the Controller, gripping his wrist and banging his hand upon the hard ground until he had released the hunting laser.

With his free hand, Regis Le Gwyn clawed at Berry's throat. He was surprisingly strong. There was a roaring in Berry's ears. Trying to ignore the pain he felt, he made a great effort and smashed his head down on the Controller's face.

The Controller grunted, twitched and lay still. Berry felt blood trickle down where his forehead had hit Regis Le Gwyn's teeth. The blood ran into his eyes and temporarily blinded him.

Twenty-nine

BERRY WIPED THE BLOOD from his face, made sure that Regis Le Gwyn was still unconscious, and saw that Tala and Vron were already making their way round the lake.

He gazed up at the homing bees, still hovering, still buzzing softly.

"People of Heaven Seven, you have seen and heard what has passed. Your Controller is alive, his companions, I fear are not. It was their lives or ours. You have seen what dirtside savages can accomplish against the best of the ristos. Think on what you have seen. Regis Le Gwyn is my prisoner. Do not send more armed men against us, or I will kill him. Also do not track us with robots or bees. I will hold your chief no more than two days. Then, if I have not achieved what I wish to achieve, I will release him unharmed in exchange for a safe conduct and a guarantee of being returned to Earth with my companions. I have spoken. Think now whether or not we of Earth are your equals in courage and intelligence."

He turned to Tala. "Laser the bees. They have served their purpose."

Regis Le Gwyn groaned and stirred. Berry lifted his head and banged it hard upon the ground.

Vron said: "Berry, why did you risk being lasered?"

Berry said: "Why did you stand up and cry out. The laser is faster than the anaesthetic dart."

"I am sorry. I thought he was going to kill you."

Berry laughed. "I thought also that he was about to kill you. Now tear strips from one of these tekno robes. We must bind this man's hands and hobble his feet. He will be in a rare temper when he regains his senses."

Berry was right. When Regis Le Gwyn recovered consciousness he groaned and breathed deeply for a few moments. Then, remembering what had happened, he uttered a great cry and struggled to sit upright. He gazed at his bound hands in dismay.

"I hope your teeth were not greatly loosened," said Berry. "They did little to improve my forehead, as you may see."

"Kill me, savage," gasped the Controller. "You have shamed me beyond endurance. But I will die knowing that you will soon follow."

"Chief, a wise man does not seek death unless he is in great pain. Only fools seek death to solve their problems."

"Then I am a fool. Laser me and let it be quick. I should have killed you when I first set eyes upon you."

"But you did not. Perhaps that was the beginning of wisdom. You are my prisoner, and it is important that we understand each other. I do not wish to kill you, unless it becomes necessary, because I shall gain nothing by the act. Do you still believe yourself to be a better man than I?"

"Yes, savage," retorted Regis Le Gwyn courageously. "You are an animal of the terrestrial forests. The life of your people is little better than the life of the animals they hunt for food. Here, in Heaven Seven, we have preserved what was left of the culture of mankind. We have the music of Beethoven, as it was played a thousand years ago. Do you know the music of Beethoven?"

"No, chief. I am ignorant of many things. But I am willing to learn."

"Have you seen a Shakespeare play? Do you understand the philosophy of Existentialism? Have you read Tolstoi, seen a Leonardo painting, watched Fonteyn dance in 'Swan Lake'? What do you know of giants such as Sartre, Ibsen, Molière, Cervantes, Eliot, Goethe? Intellectually, savage, you and your kind are in the Stone Age. You are the trash that is left after the destruction of a civilisation."

"These giants, they are very big people?" enquired Berry.

Regis Le Gwyn laughed. "Giants of the spirit, stupid one. Men whose thoughts made them immortal."

"They are of your people?"

"They lived on Earth long ago."

"Then, clearly, they were dirtside savages," said Berry with a smile. "I am surprised that they are worthy of your interest. Surely the ristos have bred giants greater than these you have named? Here in Heaven Seven you have many skills. You can cause the child of one woman to issue from the womb of another, you can manufacture robots, use atomic energy, recycle bio-material, create synthetic gravity, and perform many other wonders. Yet it seems you cannot breed giants, and you need dirtside women to bear children for your own women. Chief, I think your people are weak and vulnerable."

Regis Le Gwyn said wearily: "You cannot understand. We are the inheritors. Now kill me and be done with it."

"Chief, it would give me some pleasure to kill you, I must confess. But historical necessity dictates that I do not."

"Historical necessity?" Regis Le Gwyn looked blank.

"Yes, chief. I learned much while I was with the teknos. I learned the basic principles of mathematics, physics, astrophysics, biology. I also learned something of Earth history. I do not know the giants you have named. But I do know that, without the work of men like Kepler, Galileo, Bruno, Newton, Rutherford, Fermi, Tsiolkovsky, Oppenheimer, Einstein and von Braun, Heaven Seven would never have existed. Plato, Machiavelli, Karl Marx and Mao Tse Tung warned our common ancestors of the way the world was going. Newton, Rutherford, Einstein and von Braun — though they did not know it — ensured both the destruction and the survival of mankind. It is a good joke. Also, chief, it is exceedingly humorous that you and your kind and I and my kind are still genetically compatible."

Regis Le Gwyn looked at him wide-eyed. "Savage, I did not comprehend how much the teknos could pour into you, and how receptive you were. You amaze me."

Berry smiled. "Do not forget, also, that I have recently become a good chess player."

A magnificent deer emerged from the trees on the far side of the lake and began to graze unconcernedly. Berry gazed at it in admiration for a few moments. Then he said: "You would kill such a creature for sport, Controller. You would take pride in your deed. I would only kill it for food, and regret its passing . . . There is much that each of us may learn from the other . . . But I waste time. Come, we have some marching to do. I hope you are fit enough to travel."

"And if I refuse to move?"

"No, chief, I will not kill you. I will put the laser on its lowest power and raise many painful blisters on the non-vital parts of your body until wisdom triumphs over courage. I do not wish to inflict pain needlessly. Do you desire to test my ability to do so?"

Regis Le Gwyn struggled to his feet. He might have faced the pain, but he could not bring himself to face the humiliation of such treatment at the hands of a man he despised and hated.

"One thing is certain. You will not be allowed to remain at liberty long in Parkzone. After what has happened, robots will be programmed for homicide."

"I do not think so," said Berry cheerfully. "Your people will wait first to see if I keep my word. The bees relayed my message. I said I would release you in two days. I think the ristos will give me that time for the life of their chief."

The Controller was bewildered. "What can you hope to achieve in two days?"

"A negotiated peace between the people of Earth and the people of Heaven Seven. I am a reasonable man." Berry turned to the women. "Collect the extra hunting lasers. They are the only weapons we shall need now. The time has come for us to travel purposefully."

He went to the dead ristos and searched their clothing until he found what he was looking for: two small metal discs.

Thirty

THOUGH, AS BERRY HAD calculated, the total area of Parkzone was little more than two hundred square kilometres, it was a miracle of ecological engineering. It was divided into three ranges: the alpine range, the tropical range and the temperate range. Each range was electronically isolated from the others, so that wild life could not escape or accidentally wander from its proper territory. And each electronic wall had gates spaced at regular intervals along its length. Through these gates human beings could pass, if they possessed the authorisation discs that would actuate the gate mechanism. Berry had two such discs, taken from the dead ristos. He knew that Regis Le Gwyn possessed a third.

There was an airlock entrance into each of the three Parkzone ranges from the great tunnel that formed the axis of Heaven Seven. These entrances were used when the robots replenished the wild life with stock taken from Earth. Berry already knew that he could reach one of these entryports by marching along the length of an electronic wall. He knew also that he was at present in the temperate range and that once he had found the electronic wall, his task would be easy.

Too easy and too obvious. Something an intelligent risto might just possibly expect him to do. But if, for a time, he were to make random movements from range to range — he had no doubt that the gates would monitor his passing — there would be nothing to suggest that he knew of the existence of the great tunnel or that he hoped to enter it.

With the approach of night, Berry decided, he would try to get back into the temperate range. If no more gates were then passed, the ristos might be tricked into assuming that he had returned to the kind of country he knew best in order to make camp for the night. Berry knew that the ristos themselves would be unlikely to enter Parkzone during the hours of darkness; and even if they then decided to use bees or robots, those, too, would be hampered by lack of light. Even if they traced the fugitives, they would find it difficult to distinguish between the Controller and his enemies.

"I will take the lead," said Berry, "Regis Le Gwyn, you will march behind me. The two women will march behind you . . . Vron, you will be immediately behind the Controller. Keep your laser ready at all times. If he tries to escape or if he tries to attack me, wound him, but do not kill him. If I can, I will keep my word to the people of Heaven Seven. Tala, it is your task to warn if you think we are being observed or followed. Therefore, walk some paces behind Vron, so that the sounds we make will not greatly distract your hearing."

"Yes, my chief."

"Where are you taking me?" demanded Regis Le Gwyn.

Berry laughed. "Chief, if I were to tell you, and if you were to escape, you would think me a very simple man."

Regis Le Gwyn gave a faint smile. "I was foolish enough to think so once. It was a great mistake."

Berry said: "Let us go, then."

They marched until the sun was high. Berry knew where he was going. He wanted to get close to the perimeter before he found a gate into the next range. Those who monitored the use of the gates would hardly suspect that he would travel almost directly away from the area he most desperately wanted to reach.

A thought suddenly struck him. He silently cursed himself for a fool that he had not considered the possibility before. What if the space ship were not in the docking tunnel? What if it had journeyed down to Earth once more for another cargo of dirtside females? He could not change his plan now — indeed, he could think of no other plan. It was a risk he would simply have to accept. He still had the Controller in his hands; and if he could reach the docking tunnel, he might discover a way of working it. That would give him almost as much negotiating strength as if he had possession of the space vessel.

The day was warm and pleasant. As he led the way through the forests of the temperate range, disturbing deer, game birds and even the occasional wild boar, Berry wondered if it would occur to the people of Heaven Seven that they might gain some advantage by changing the climatic programme of Parkzone. But, then, he reflected, the power to do so lay not in the hands of the ristos but in the hands of the teknos. At the moment, he judged, the situation between the ristos and the teknos must be very tense. The teknos would have been blamed entirely for Berry's escape and its consequences. Berry did not forget that Regis Le Gwyn had charged him with conspiring with the Programmer — perhaps not only because he believed it to be true but also because he wished to divert attention from his own inadequacies and channel any discontent towards the teknos — and the bees had relayed the exchange to the people of Heaven Seven. Berry hoped that the teknos were not under too much pressure. No doubt, many powerful ristos were now demanding that the teknos find some way of immediately securing the safety of the Controller. But Bors Zangwin was a good chess player . . .

Presently, Berry saw the gleaming metal bars of the electronic wall in the distance, not more than a kilometre away. The sun had passed its zenith. He judged it was a good time to rest and take food. The forest had been left behind, they were now in open grassland, and the nearest gate to the tropical range could not be very far away.

Suddenly, he was aware of noises behind. He turned and saw several startled deer emerging from the forest. Birds rose above the trees complaining mightily. This could mean only one thing.

Berry turned to Regis Le Gwyn. "Lie quietly in the grass, chief, else I will burn the hands from your wrists." He motioned to Tala and Vron, who also lay down.

Regis Le Gwyn did as he was ordered. But, when he spoke to Berry, he could not restrain the note of triumph in his voice. "My people seek me, savage. You can not stand against them long."

Berry was glad that the grass was high. "Chief, I warned your people that, if they hunted us, I would kill you. But this I should have expected. It seems there are some who would find your death convenient."

"Berry, you are a fool. My friends come to liberate me regardless of personal danger."

Berry sighed. "Chief, they do not intend to liberate you but to kill you, or to see you killed. It is thus with the clans of Earth. When the people believe that a chief has made too many mistakes, they compel him to embrace the daggers, and a new chief is found. These — your friends, as you call them — do not hunt dirtside savages, they hunt you."

Regis Le Gwyn laughed. "Now I know that you are a fool, despite the training given you by the teknos. We are a civilised people. My friends seek me at risk of their own lives."

Berry sighed. "Chief, you have much to learn."

Five men emerged from the forest line, all ristos by their garb. They carried hunting lasers. They advanced purposefully and cautiously, as if they knew where the fugitives were hiding.

Berry was immensely surprised. He had not expected the ristos to be such good trackers. Then he understood.

"You carry a micro-transmitter, Controller?" It was more a statement than a question.

Regis Le Gwyn said nothing; but his very silence was confirmation.

The pursuing ristos were now less than four hundred metres away. They moved cautiously, slowly, no doubt aware from the strength of the signal that they could not be far from the source.

"There is still time to throw the transmitter away, chief. The grass is tall. Before they reach us, we shall be able to crawl far enough to one side to surprise them."

"Savage, the game is played out. You may yet kill me, but your own fate is sealed."

Berry said: "I gave my word to your people. I will still try to keep it. But in return, I require something. I require that you will not stand up or make any sound until your friends are very close. I must still do my best for myself and these women."

The Controller looked at him in surprise. "A dirtside savage with integrity! What wonders shall I see next? Very well, in return for my life I give you until my friends are within fifty paces. And there will be no more bargains. After that, I, too, will hunt you."

"If you live, chief," retorted Berry drily. Silently, he beckoned Vron and Tala. The three of them began to crawl through the high grass, disturbing it as little as possible. They carried their hunting lasers ready at maximum power. There was no sound from Regis Le Gwyn. He also was demonstrating that he could keep his word.

When Berry judged that the ristos were near to where the Controller lay, he signalled to the women to stop. Cautiously, he raised his head so that he could see between the tops of the grasses.

He was in time to see Regis Le Gwyn stand up and wave his bound hands gaily over the top of his head. The five ristos were less than forty metres from him.

He shouted to them. "Karil, Jorn, Ulros — well met. Yura, Solon, it is good to see you. I am unharmed, as you see."

"Where are the animals, Regis?"

The Controller shrugged. "They panicked when they saw you, and fled. They cannot be far away. Come, loose these bonds, and we will hunt them together."

"You are sure they fled?" called one of the ristos.

"Man, would I say so if it were otherwise?" demanded the Controller irritably. "They are familiar with the ways of the forest. You drove the deer before you, and gave them much warning."

"So, the problem is simplified," said the risto calmly. "We can hunt them at our leisure."

"Don't waste time, then," snapped the Controller. "Get these miserable strips of cloth from my wrists and legs, Karil."

"I am sorry, Regis," said the one addressed as Karil. "It is necessary for you to die."

The Controller gazed at him speechless for a moment or two. Then he said icily: "This is no time for humour. Jorn, Ulros, loosen me."

No one moved.

Karil went on: "Bors Zangwin has released the results of his tests upon the savage, Regis. He is a highly intelligent and gifted man — as was demonstrated by your disastrous encounter with him a few hours ago. It was very stupid of you to be so confident of your ability and to have the bees there ready to relay the incident. Afterwards, the savage guaranteed your life in return for time — to accomplish what I do not know. The nilskils — and many ristos, even — are now saying that it is morally wrong for us to exploit such intelligent people, little realising that if we do not continue to use dirtside females our very future is at risk. As things now stand, we ristos are discredited, Regis. We have held power for a long time; but now — thanks to your inadequacy — the nilskils, who greatly outnumber us, as you know, are no longer in a mood to accept, unquestioningly, risto authority. And the teknos are beginning to influence them towards the outmoded concept of democracy . . . All this has been brought about by your stupidity, Regis. You should have killed the savage when you first set eyes on him. You are not fit to govern . . . But, if it is known that you have been lasered by the savage, people will realise that, though the savage and his kind may be intelligent, they are vicious and cannot be trusted. We shall be able to restore the authority of the ristos, and we shall be able to continue to use the dirtside females to bear our children. Also, I think, the tide will turn against Bors Zangwin and his stupid notions of equality. . . A man has a right to know why he must die, Regis. I hope I have explained the reason adequately. I am sorry you must finish trussed like an animal. But we must be able to show that dirtside creatures are naturally depraved, whatever their Q ratings."

Regis Le Gwyn looked at the others. "I take it that Karil speaks for you all?"

One of them said: "Regis, it is the only way. Your death is necessary."

Surprisingly, Regis Le Gwyn laughed. "A friend warned me that this would happen. I did not believe him. As you say, I am not fit to govern . . . But who will be the next Controller, Karil? Will it be you?"

"We shall hold an election, Regis."

Again Regis Le Gwyn laughed. "Ah, yes. I know about elections . . . Well, do not waste time, gentlemen. Let us conclude this little comedy. After you have killed me, you will have to hunt the savage and his two dirtside women. That will be interesting. The man has higher Q ratings than even Bors Zangwin supposed."

Berry, lying in the grass, had heard most of the exchange. The air was still and, though a slight breeze had robbed him of a few words, for the most part he had heard clearly.

When the ristos raised their hunting lasers, Berry beamed the nearest, burning his head from his shoulders. Momentarily, the remaining four froze in shock.

Still concealed in the tall grasses, Berry shouted: "Whoever moves dies! Whoever drops his laser lives."

One risto half turned; Berry beamed him instantly. The remaining three dropped their weapons.

Berry motioned to Vron and Tala to remain concealed and to cover him. Then he stood up and advanced.

"I am a poor dirtside savage," he said, "but I try to keep my word. The Controller of Heaven Seven is my prisoner. I have said that he will be released unharmed in return for certain guarantees. Go back to Citizone, ristos. Tell anyone who enquires that I killed two of your company because they broke the truce and attacked me. But say nothing more. Your lives may depend upon it." He smiled. "Better your friends die than that I should kill the Controller. They and you will be regarded as brave men."

The three surviving ristos gazed at him in horror and amazement.

Regis Le Gwyn gave a grim laugh. "I am not alone, I see, in underestimating the dirtside savage. It occurs to me, also, that I have less to fear from my enemy than from my friends. Do as he says. He has led a hard life and has survived long on a world where such as you and I would not last a day. He knows how to kill, as you have seen. But he kills of necessity only — something we have yet to learn. He has given you your lives. Go. And let all of us bury in our minds for ever what has just happened."

"These are the words of your chief," said Berry, "who, in adversity, displays courage and wisdom. Obey him. I have no time for argument."

The three ristos said nothing. They could not meet the gaze of the Controller, nor could they face Berry.

As they made their way back to the forest, Regis Le Gwyn turned to Berry and said: "My friend, it seems I must thank you. I am learning, at last, that I have much to learn."

"Chief," retorted Berry, "I am not your friend. I am an alien in your world, and you are my prisoner . . . We have much travelling to do. Let us eat now, and restore our strength."

Vron and Tala emerged from the long grasses.

"Why did you not let us kill them all, Berry?" asked Vron.

"Woman," said Berry, "dead men are useless. Those who live may advance our cause. The ristos have again been defeated. Let them carry the news of their defeat. Now we will rest awhile and take food."

Thirty-one

THE MICRO-TRANSMITTER THAT REGIS LE GWYN
carried, and that had almost brought about his death, was
in a tiny hexagonal case — clearly designed to look like
some kind of adornment — that had been clipped into
the Controller's thick hair. Regis Le Gwyn surrendered
the device without any sign of reluctance. No doubt he
was reflecting that it had very nearly brought about his
destruction.

"You will destroy it?" he asked indifferently.

Berry thought for a moment or two. Then he said
enigmatically: "No, chief, I will use it." He slipped the
device into his pocket.

The electronic walls that separated the ranges of Parkzone from each other, consisted of rows of thin metal
bars which automatically began to grow hot whenever
and wherever they were approached. Normally, the heat
radiated was sufficient to drive back any person or any
creature when it was more than a metre from the barrier.
But if the person or animal still came closer, the bars
glowed fiercely and brilliantly. Experimentally, Berry
came as close as fifty centimetres to the wall, but had to
draw back almost instantly because of the pain in his
eyes and on his skin, and because the fabric of his clothing began to smoulder.

"Let us find the first gate," he said. "The watchers
must be rewarded for their patience."

With the two additional discs taken from the dead

ristos, Berry now had five keys to operate the inter-range gates. The spare disc, he thought, might be useful; though at present he did not know how.

Throughout a long afternoon, he made his little party march many weary kilometres, passing from range to range through the gates. Many times he glanced anxiously at Vron, the weakest of the four. Her face looked drawn and pale; but she did not complain. She was a strong woman, he knew. Presently, if all went well, she would have ample time to rest. Also, if things went ill, she would rest eternally.

The gates were — though Berry did not know it — merely a sophisticated version of the ancient revolving door. A person wishing to pass from one range to another simply stood on a small platform, inserted his disc in the scanning mechanism, then waited for the platform to rotate and his disc was returned to him.

The tropical range was filled with wonders. Berry marvelled at the strange and beautiful birds that noisily squawked and called in trees whose foliage was dense enough to shut out the light of the sun. He saw creatures he had never seen before: monkeys effortlessly swinging from branch to branch; lizards and scaly creatures that looked very formidable; huge butterflies, water creatures that reeked of evil and death. Once he had to laser a great serpent that seemed to drop from nowhere and coil itself around Tala.

The humidity and heat of the tropical range caused everyone to sweat profusely. Vron pleaded to be allowed to discard her heavy robe. Berry refused. Regis Le Gwyn tried stoically — and failed — to ignore the mosquitoes and flies. Tala whimpered occasionally, but said nothing.

It was a relief to pass into the alpine range. At least, at first it was a relief. The clean, cool air; the rocky, snow-covered slopes; the chamois and the eagles; the stunted pine trees — all these seemed like a kind of liberation after the death-laden primordial rain forests.

But presently everyone was shivering. Berry gazed in awe at the man-made splendour of artificial hills, at the snow and ice whose occurrence was regulated with precision by a controlled heat loss from the base and dome of Heaven Seven. The people of this island in the sky, he thought, may be weak and vulnerable in some respects. But the fact that they had achieved all this showed that they had in them the seeds of greatness. If only their skills and ingenuity could be harnessed to the immense fund of human energy that now existed on Earth . . .

"Well, savage, have you seen enough of Parkzone?" The Controller's teeth were rattling with the cold.

"Yes, chief, I have seen enough," said Berry tranquilly. Ice was forming on his eyebrows, but he did not care. "You of Heaven Seven are a great people. Now let us go back."

Regis Le Gwyn shrugged wearily. He had become wiser and more chastened in the past few hours. He tried to shut from his mind the memory of that first encounter with Berry. But he could not. He recalled his own arrogance and pride. He recalled how he had been compelled to terminate the interview by putting a laser hole in the savage's leg.

An ordinary man would have been unable to resist the temptation to revenge himself when the opportunity arose. Yet Berry had saved his life. Perhaps he planned a more subtle revenge. Regis Le Gwyn had gained wisdom in that he now knew himself to be a proud, over-confident and egotistical man. He had gained knowledge of himself, but not of Berry. The man remained an enigma.

Thirty-two

THE JOURNEY BACK TO the temperate range was exhausting. Frequent stops had to be made while Vron and Tala rested. On one such stop in the tropical range, Regis Le Gwyn was moved to pick two beautiful white flowers which he presented to the women. At first he did not know why he had made the gesture. Then he knew. It was an apology. It was an apology on behalf of the people of Heaven Seven to the women of Earth. An apology for centuries of exploitation.

Vron looked at her orchid in wonder. She had never seen such a flower — beautiful, exotic, sensuous. Tala pinned her bloom into her hair.

"Thank you, Lord," said Tala softly. "You honour us."

"I know not how to say this," began Regis Le Gwyn.

Berry cut him short. "Chief, you have already said it. I thank you. The gesture was a fine one. My people understand."

"Berry, you are a very strange man. I thought you to be no better than an animal. I was wrong. I realise you have your reasons for making this long march, but your women are tired. Let them rest. Use your transceiver to get help. Robots can be here in less than an hour. I will guarantee your safe return to Earth."

"Chief, I thank you for your courtesy, and I believe you," said Berry. "But I play for higher stakes. I will do my best for the women. This they understand. But I have a plan that is worth hazarding our lives for. If it fails, and if we live, I shall be humble enough to remind you of your offer."

The Controller sighed. "Then will you unbind my hands and remove these tiresome rags from my feet?"

"I am sorry, chief. The stakes are too high for me to accept an additional risk. Let us go now. The women are rested."

The sun was very low by the time they had returned to the temperate range. Berry insisted that they come back through the gate they had first entered.

They rested by a stream, drank its cool water gratefully, ate some more of the food concentrate. Berry gave each of the women one of the tiny capsules that blocked awareness of fatigue, and took one himself. He did not offer one to Regis Le Gwyn. Better that the Controller remained aware of his tiredness.

Berry waited for the stimulant to work, then he said: "It is almost time for us to travel once more." He glanced at the sky. "There is, I think, enough daylight left for us to march eight or nine kilometres. Tala, Vron, I shall leave you for a short time. Do not approach the Controller. Do not let him approach you. If he moves, laser his arm if you need to restrain him; but try not to hurt him greatly."

Regis Le Gwyn smiled. "Berry, you continually surprise me."

Berry said: "Sometimes, chief, I even surprise myself."

He was not gone long. He ran back to the gate to the tropical range and inserted the spare authorisation disc. But he did not pass through. He hoped that whoever monitored the use of the gates would believe that someone had passed through. If so, it would add to their confusion. They would not know whether the Controller had escaped, whether Berry himself had gone back into the tropical range alone, or whether one of the women had been used as a decoy.

When he returned, Berry was relieved to see that all was well. The Controller lay tranquilly on his back, gazing up at the cloud-flecked sky, while Tala watched him with great concentration and Vron also rested on her back.

Berry took the micro-transmitter from his pocket and left it on the grass. Even if the use of the gates had not been monitored, it was almost certain that their journeyings had been traced through the device that Regis Le Gwyn had carried in his hair. If the micro-transmitter now remained stationary, it could suggest that, after an exhausting day of looking fruitlessly for an unmonitored exit from Parkzone, Berry had decided to camp for the night.

But those who tracked the movement of the transmitter could not be sure that it remained in the possession of Regis Le Gwyn. Which, if they had monitored the apparently solitary use of one gate, should puzzle them even more.

It was rather like a game of chess, thought Berry, where one of the players was blindfolded, relying on someone to tell him which moves had been made. The gates between the ranges would tell of certain moves, as would the movement of the transmitter. The blindfold player, thought Berry, pursuing the analogy, had many pieces at his disposal; whereas his opponent had only two pawns and a knight — and, of course, the king. But the position of those four pieces could not be known. An interesting contest . . .

If, indeed, any such contest existed. It might well be that Berry was wasting his time; that, apart from the ristos who had tried to kill Regis Le Gwyn, the people of Heaven Seven had given him the time he requested.

But Berry was a cautious man. He did not think his elaborate precautions had been in vain.

"Now we march north," he said. "We will keep close to the electronic wall, and we will travel as before. I will lead, chief. You will follow. As always, there will be a laser at your back."

"North?" enquired Regis Le Gwyn blankly.

"North," repeated Berry. He seemed surprised that the Controller had not already guessed the destination. "So far, chief, we have played amusing but exhausting games for the benefit of your people. They tracked us. At least, I hope they tracked us. If they did, they would perhaps deduce that caged animals were moving at random. If they did not track our movements, so much the better. They will not know that we are now heading for the axis, the great tunnel."

And then Regis Le Gwyn understood.

Thirty-three

THE FIRST STARS WERE out by the time Berry found the entrance to the great tunnel. It had taken longer than he had thought; but there was still enough light to see by. He hoped the weather programme for Heaven Seven included a moonlit night.

Everyone was showing signs of fatigue — Berry estimated that they had travelled more than forty kilometres during the course of the day — but, for the present, Regis Le Gwyn was the only person to be aware of his fatigue. Still, it was something to have reached the entrance of the great tunnel.

It was something — and it was nothing.

The high, almost hemispherical door was of metal — hiduminium by the feel of it, but it could be steel — and there were no means of opening it from the outside.

The door was at the base of an almost vertical rock face. Berry surmised that the rock was merely a covering for the metallic structure of the tunnel complex. He tried to find out whether the door was designed to rise or to slide to one side. The grooving at its base did not enlighten him; though he thought it probable that the door lifted.

He tried to laser a hole in the metal. He put the hunting laser on maximum power and concentrated on one spot for about five seconds. The metal glowed red, then amber, then white. But it did not melt. Nevertheless he had learned something. The door was not of hiduminium but of steel.

"Stalemate," said Regis Le Gwyn.

"Perhaps," said Berry. "I must think. Your offer of a safe conduct still holds, chief?"

"Until daybreak, Berry. I admire your spirit, but I must be practical."

Berry grinned. "Chief, we must each be practical. Until daybreak, then. Meanwhile, your life is still in my hands. Do not be rash."

The weather programme for Heaven Seven did include a moonlit night. The moon showed over the tree line and cast a cold glow on the impenetrable door.

"What now?" asked Vron.

"I do not know. I must think. It is hard to believe that we have achieved so much and should now be stopped by a metal door." He hit it with his fist. There was a faint rattle as the door moved slightly on its bearings. Clearly, the steel was not very thick. Berry sighed with exasperation.

He sighed; but he felt like shouting, kicking, stamping. He wanted to express his frustration in some kind of violent action. But there were times, he knew, when a chief could not permit himself to express his emotions. This was one of those times. Tala and Vron depended upon him. He felt defeated. But that was something they must not know.

"Do not despair, chief," said Tala. "The Controller has promised to return us to our own land. Is that not enough?"

"No, it is not enough!" he shouted. "It is not enough for the clans of Earth or for the women taken from those clans and made to bear the children of others." He glanced at the Controller. "Perhaps that man will give us our lives. I do not know. But, whether he does or not, the ristos will continue to send their robots to take our women. And in the end, we will be destroyed. Without Earth women, this island in the sky is doomed. Are the ristos a people who will tranquilly face their own extinction?" He glared at the Controller. "Speak the truth, chief. Say if your women will be prepared to let their bodies grow fat, to bring forth abnormal babies, to lose their youth and their beauty?"

"Berry," said Regis Le Gwyn, "you have lived long enough under the harsh conditions of your world to know that victory goes to the strong. It is a principle of evolution. Even if you kill me now, the people of Heaven Seven will continue to take what they need in order to survive. Every species has the right to survive — if it can."

"Including," said Berry, "the entire human race." He turned to Tala. "Take the Controller a little way from here. Let him rest, but watch him carefully . . . I must think."

The moonlight, now quite strong, bathed the steel door in silver. If only it were silver, thought Berry wistfully. The laser would cut through it easily. But though the theoretical temperature of the laser beam was high enough to melt steel, the heat loss caused by conductivity and radiation prevented it.

Out of the corner of his eye, Berry noted that the Controller was now stretched out against a grassy mound with Tala some short distance away, watching him intently.

"Berry," said Vron hesitantly, "with the hunting lasers taken from the dead ristos, we now have five weapons. I know little of such things, but I have seen how powerful these weapons are. Might it not be that —"

"Woman!" shouted Berry. "I am a fool. I should have thought of this thing."

"Chief," said Vron, smiling, "you have had to think of so much."

Experimentally, with a hunting laser in each hand, Berry focused the maximum power beams upon the same spot on the door. The metal glowed white-hot, but it did not melt.

But, with Vron using two more lasers, the concentrated energy of the four beams converging on the same mark brought the steel to a white heat instantly and caused it to spit and drip.

"Enough!" said Berry. He peered closely at the small hole. "We are through." Hurriedly he searched on the ground for a sharp piece of stone. When he found one, he used it to scratch a curved line at the base of the door. If the segment of metal could be cut out, it would leave a hole big enough for a man to crawl through.

"We will start here," he said, pointing. "As the metal drips away, we will move our laser beams along the line. Are your hands steady, Vron? The laser beams must all be kept together."

"I will make them steady. Let us begin."

It was a long business. The brilliant whiteness of the melting steel half-blinded both of them. The heat made them sweat profusely and brought unfelt blisters to their faces. They both had to blink frequently to protect their aching and streaming eyes. But, somehow, they managed to keep the four beams focused on the same slowly moving point.

One hunting laser died when they were no more than a few centimetres from the end of the curve Berry had scratched. Then another died, its micropile exhausted. The metal of the door stopped dripping and merely glowed.

Berry stood back. He lay down on his belly and

examined the cut. It was clean. Except for the last six or seven centimetres.

"Go to Tala," he said. "Draw her away from Regis Le Gwyn and change her laser for a spent one. Do not let him see this. You understand?"

"I understand."

Presently Vron returned with an almost fully charged laser.

"We no longer have the heat to melt," said Berry. "But we still have the heat to weaken. Use your lasers when I give the word. I will push."

Berry found two rocks which he grasped to protect himself from the heat of the steel. He pressed them against the segment of metal. "Burn!"

Vron played the beams slowly along the remaining obstinate centimetres of steel. Berry thrust hard with the rocks against the segment of door. Slowly the last few centimetres of inert steel turned red, then amber. Berry thrust and thrust with the rocks against the door. He could feel the sharp stone edges cutting into the palms of his hands. He could feel blood and sweat mingling on his wrists, but he did not care. The pain seemed, somehow, irrelevant.

Slowly the metal gave. Slowly, the segment was pressed inwards. Grunting and snarling and gasping, Berry continued to thrust until the semi-circular piece of metal was about at right angles to the door. Then, suddenly, there was a dull crack; and the metal fractured where Vron lasered it. The piece of door that had been cut away with such effort fell noisily inwards in the tunnel.

Berry lay on his stomach gasping and groaning for a while. He let the rocks fall from his bloodstained hands; and a wave of agony swept over him. But presently, he recovered himself. He stood up and wiped his hands gently on his torn tekno robe. He wondered if he could hold a laser. There was still some power left in three of the weapons.

He winced as he handled the laser; but the important fact was that he could still hold it and use it.

"The game is not yet played," he called to Regis Le Gwyn. "Follow closely, Controller. Remember always the laser that is behind you."

Thirty-four

THE CORRIDOR WAS WIDE and well-lighted. There was a strange scent. Berry sniffed and diagnosed the lingering smell of animals. Here and there on the floor were faint stains — doubtless caused by animal droppings as the terrified creatures were driven into Parkzone by the robots.

As he hurried along, Berry's spirits rose. At least he had got into the axis. Was it too much to hope that the space vessel would be accessible?

The corridor was long — perhaps two hundred metres. Almost half way down it, there were two electromagnetically locked doors, one on each side. Berry paused to inspect them. The locking mechanism seemed similar to those of the doors in Faczone.

He sped on to the end of the corridor and came to a halt in front of a formidable steel door with no opening mechanism visible. His new-found hope died rapidly. The door — probably leading through some kind of air-lock to the vessel's entry port — was obviously too massive to yield to his seriously diminished reserves of laser power.

Regis Le Gwyn shrugged. "Still stalemate, I think, Berry."

"Not while I live!" he snapped.

He brushed past the Controller and sped back to the locked side doors. There should be enough laser energy to open one of those, at least.

He looked for some indication on the wall that would tell him where the locking circuitry was buried. He could find none. He would have to work by trial and error. It took five precious laser blasts before he heard the muffled click that told him the electromagnet had released the locking rod.

He pushed the door open and entered the new corridor. It was smaller than the one he had just left. Also it curved. There was no smell of animals. Berry beckoned impatiently to Regis Le Gwyn. Using her laser, Tala pushed the Controller through the doorway.

There were several doors at regular intervals along the inner wall of the corridor, but none on the outer. Each of the doors had handles. He opened one door and saw what was evidently some kind of store room for electronic components. He opened another and was instantly terrified by what looked like a row of motionless robots. Then he remembered fragments of space technology from his crash training — and identified them as space suits. Why would the robots need space suits? They would not — but the teknos would if they wished to venture outside the dome or inspect the hull of their space vessel.

He opened several other doors, and found only store chambers of one kind or another and an automated engineering workshop. Berry resumed his exploration of the long, curved corridor. He carried his laser nervously at the ready, expecting at any moment to meet service robots. But he did not encounter any.

Finally, the corridor led to a lift. The control panel had studs for ten levels; but there was nothing to indicate what he might expect to find on those levels.

"Chief, have you been here before?" he asked Regis Le Gwyn.

The Controller said: "I have never concerned myself

184

with mechanical matters. That is the province of the teknos and the robots."

"It is the duty of a chief to familiarise himself with all that he governs," said Berry.

On impulse, he punched the stud for level five. The lift doors opened. He motioned the Controller to enter.

Level five was a place of vibration and heat. A place also where there were many service robots and two or three teknos supervising large banks of instruments. The vast, curved chamber literally hummed with energy. Before he leaped back into the lift, hastily punching another stud, Berry realised that he had just seen a power plant where the heat produced by atomic energy was converted into electricity. He hoped that he had not been seen. He thought not. The robots and the teknos had been intent upon their duties.

Berry looked at the stud he had just pressed. Level ten. Well, perhaps it was a good thing to go to the top. It was as good a place to go as any.

The lift doors opened, revealing a large chamber, from which yet another corridor ran off. There were three robots in the chamber.

One carried some electronic equipment, trailing multi-coloured leads, another held what looked like a transparent sphere with many points of light twinkling inside it, the third carried several coils of bright metal. They were all coming towards the lift.

Berry lasered the vision circuits of one. Vron missed her target and seared the wall behind it. Berry lasered the one she had missed and then hit the third. Still clutching their burdens, the robots staggered about blindly.

Berry thought of trying to put out of action their communication circuits and movement systems. But then he rejected the notion. He did not know how much laser energy there was left.

Even now, he realised, they were raising the alarm. It could not be helped. Should he try another level, or should he explore the corridor at the far end of the chamber?

He did not know. He was tired, he was dispirited, he was confused. But a decision had to be made. It was the duty of a chief to make decisions.

"Follow me. Ignore the robots. They cannot see to harm us or prevent us. Keep away from them, that is all. Tala, if the Controller hesitates, burn him." He ran towards the corridor.

It was not a long one. Part way down it, Berry noticed that the floors and walls stopped and were joined to the next stretch by a tough, flexible, metallic fabric. A few paces farther on, there was another break and another flexible join. Was it an illusion, or had the floor of the corridor seemed to sway slightly as he ran down it?

He had no time to answer the question before he burst into a chamber containing many consoles of instruments and some circular transparent panels high in its metallic walls. He looked back to assure himself that the others had followed. He saw two studs on the wall near the opening where they had entered. One shone, one was dark. He pressed the one that shone. Noiselessly, a panel moved and the opening was closed. He heard a hiss of air, then several clicks.

At least, for the time being, pursuit was cut off.

Berry looked up through one of the circular panels. He saw stars. Stars in a black sky. And the stars were moving. They rotated slowly, as if engaging in some strange ritual dance. Berry was dumbfounded. The stars could not move like that. Not the real stars, nor the synthetic stars of Heaven Seven.

Then he understood. And he laughed. He laughed

until the tears streamed down his face. It was a good joke.

"Berry, my chief, my love, are you well?" asked Vron anxiously.

"Yes," he laughed, "I am well. And the day has gone well. Be not afraid."

"Let me share your joke, Berry," said Regis Le Gwyn.

Berry wiped his eyes. "It is my pleasure, chief. Look up at the stars."

The Controller gazed up through one of the observation panels uncomprehendingly. "Something has gone wrong with the programme," he muttered. "They cannot move like that."

"No, chief, they cannot. So what conclusion do you draw?"

"Something has gone wrong with the projection programme," said Regis Le Gwyn weakly.

"Chief," said Berry, enjoying himself, "if the stars should not move like that — neither the real stars nor the stars you project upon the dome of Heaven Seven, there is a simple solution.

"The stars are not rotating. *We* are rotating. Heaven Seven must rotate on its axis to preserve its orbital attitude. Those are real stars, Regis Le Gwyn, and we are at the axis. In fact, we are now on the navigation deck of your space vessel. Look around you, man. Look at the instrumentation."

He took the transceiver he had so carefully carried throughout the long day and set it for transmission on the open distress circuit. He pressed its aerial against the hull of the space vessel.

"I am Berry, chief of the Londos clan," he said. "To the people of Heaven Seven, I speak again. I have captured your Controller, as you already know. Now I have taken possession of your space vessel. I cannot operate it.

But I can bring its atomic engines to critical mass, thus destroying both the vessel and Heaven Seven itself. We of Earth do not wish to be in conflict with you. Nor can we take any satisfaction in the destruction of a race that can give so much to a world which once nurtured its ancestors. Therefore, I offer you friendship and help on the following terms . . ."

Regis Le Gwyn, with Tala pointing her useless hunting laser unwaveringly at him, listened to the terms. He stared at Berry like a man in a trance, listening to words that — one way or another — would irrevocably change the destinies of what were, in effect, two entire worlds.

The terms were simple — and devastating. There was to be no more forcible removal of the women of Earth. For a limited time only, volunteers might be sought to serve as proxy wombs. But none must be asked to submit to more than two pregnancies, and while they were in Heaven Seven they must have rights equal to those of the nilskils, and the right to be educated. Further, exchanges must be made between the people of Heaven Seven and those of Earth. Suitable clansmen must be brought up to Faczone to learn what they could of science and technology, teknos must descend to Earth to set up training schools for children. Robots also must be sent to Earth to help construct a city complex where, eventually, Heavenside people would live, making the culture they had saved from the past available to the peoples of Earth so that in time a new civilisation would rise again.

"We of Earth are by your standards ignorant savages," went on Berry. "We are people of the forest who live simply and are prey to many diseases. But we have great energy, and many of us are eager to learn. You of Heaven Seven can give us so much. You can teach us once more the meaning of civilisation. We of Earth can give you in return something of great value. We can give you survival. We need each other. Together we can lift mankind to greatness once more ... I do not wish to destroy the space vessel or the people who have created this great island in the sky. But, remember that if I am compelled to do so, the people of Earth will still endure. And, in their own time, they will recreate what has been lost. Think on these things. Time runs short. I have spoken the truth. Let there be no deception between us. I am an ignorant man in some things. But I am cunning in others, as you must know."

Berry did not have to wait long for his answer. He recognised the voice of Bors Zangwin immediately.

"In the absence of the Controller, and by the authority vested in me by his deputies, I, Bors Zangwin, Programmer and acting Controller, agree to your requests — with the following provisos. One: the Controller will be released unharmed upon the successful conclusion of these negotiations."

"Agreed," said Berry.

"Two. Earth women already in Heaven Seven will not be returned to Earth until they have undergone the two pregnancies you stipulated."

"Agreed," said Berry. "With the exception of the women of the Londos clan. They will be returned immediately. It is a matter of politics, Programmer. Before I can persuade other clans, I need to have the backing of my own."

"Agreed," said Bors Zangwin. "The Londos women will be returned forthwith." He hesitated. "Many of them may now carry proxy children. Do you wish these to be aborted?"

Berry was silent for a while. He looked anxiously at Vron and Tala. Vron shook her head, slowly. "Let us not destroy their children," she said softly. She was still aware of the agony of losing one of her own.

"No abortions required. The children they carry will be born on Earth and will be reared on Earth. Agreed?"

"Agreed," said Bors Zangwin. "Item three. No inhabitant of Heaven Seven who is judged medically to be unable to accept the increased gravity shall be required to go to Earth."

"Agreed," said Berry.

"The fourth and last item. May I speak freely with Regis Le Gwyn?"

"You may, Programmer."

"Before I do so . . . Went the day well, Berry?"

"Chief, we are all alive. That is enough . . . Has Project Catalyst lived up to your expectations?"

"Berry, my friend, I seem to have underestimated you. Need I say more?"

Berry laughed. "Chief, I must confess that there were anxious moments. Now speak to the Controller."

"Well, Regis Le Gwyn. You are unharmed, I hope?"

"Yes, Programmer, I am unharmed. Thank you for your concern . . . Did you mean it to end like this?"

"Controller, we both know that Heaven Seven was operating on the law of diminishing returns."

Regis Le Gwyn sighed. "It is the end of an era."

"It is also the beginning of a new one. The planet Earth waits for us to make it great once more. Can you see that?"

"I can see it. In the past few hours, you will be amused to know, I have learned much from a dirtside savage."

"So have we all, Controller. So have we all."

Berry had listened to the exchange, but he had also been gazing up through the transparent panels at the rotating stars.

'Some day,' he thought, 'we of Earth will reach out to

you. Some day, the clans of Earth will become one clan only. There will be no more wars. And the seed of man will be scattered among distant worlds.'

It was a fanciful thought. Perhaps he was mad, or weak and suffering from delusions. But, he told himself, a man cannot live without dreams.

He glanced at Vron, and could see that she was already thinking of her return to the Londos settlement. He glanced at Tala. He knew that her thoughts were centred on the return to Earth also.

"Such is the nature of woman," he said, without anyone knowing his meaning. "And such is the nature of man. And between them, they bring the visions of Earth and the visions of the stars together."

He did not truly understand what he had just said. But he thought — he hoped — that one day he might understand.

BSFA